Also by Malorie Blackman

Hacker
Operation Gadgetman!
Thief!
A.N.T.I.D.O.T.E.
Pig-Heart Boy
Dangerous Reality
Hostage
Cloud Busting
The Deadly Dare Mysteries
Noughts & Crosses
Knife Edge
Check Mate
Double Cross
Dead Gorgeous
The Stuff of Nightmares
Boys Don't Cry
Trust Me
Jon for Short
Noble Conflict

Tell Me No Lies

Lies

MALORIE
BLACKMAN

MACMILLAN CHILDREN'S BOOKS

For Neil and Elizabeth, with love,
and for Sarah Davies, with thanks

First published 1999 by Macmillan Children's Books

This edition published 2006 by Macmillan Children's Books
an imprint of Pan Macmillan
20 New Wharf Road, London N1 9RR
Associated companies throughout the world
www.panmacmillan.com

ISBN 978-0-330-44623-5

22

A CIP catalogue record for this book is available from
the British Library.

Typeset by Intype Libra Ltd
Printed and bound by CPI Group (UK) Ltd, Croydon CR0 4YY

Gemma
Scrapbook

The moon and stars and rainbows on the ceiling flickered, then steadied themselves. Gemma glanced up unconcerned. She looked across her room to where her mother's scarf lay draped over the bedside lamp. The lamplight shining through the navy-blue scarf adorned with gold and silver planets, the moon and stars, made her room appear mystical, magical.

Gemma turned back to the scrapbook lying on her lap. The shaded lamp made the room dark and mysterious but there was just enough light to see by comfortably. Gemma stroked the lettering on the outside of the scrapbook before opening it. Scrapbook number seven. This book was one of her favourites and she returned to it again and again. Like all her scrapbooks, it contained photographs of mums. Mums smiling, crying, laughing, wistful. Lots and lots and lots of mums.

Gemma turned the page. Here, a mum with smiling eyes and untidy hair like a halo hugged her daughter tight, whilst the headline below the photograph yelled out, MOTHER SAVES CHILD FROM OVERTURNED CAR. And on the opposite page, a mum standing next to a boy, her arm around his shoulders. The headline that went with this photograph declared, MUM FLIES OFF WITH SON FOR NEW HEART. Gemma only ever kept the headlines that went with her mums – never the full newspaper article – but she could remember the story that went with this one. This mum's son needed a heart and liver transplant and the doctors in Britain had all but written him off. But not his mum. His mum was determined to do whatever it took to keep her son alive, so she'd taken him to America. And it had had a happy ending. The boy received his transplant and lived.

Gemma sighed. She liked happy endings. She turned the page.

'Don't shout at me, Dad. I'm not deaf!' Tarwin, Gemma's brother, yelled from downstairs.

'I'll shout at you until you start listening to what I say!' Dad ranted.

Gemma turned to the next page.

'I'll listen when you stop nagging me.'

Tarwin and Dad were at it again. Every evening they had a shouting match, a contest to see who could raise the roof first.

Ah! Now here was a mum who looked lovely. She had kind, twinkling eyes. She was a foster mum whom everyone loved. She never said a cross word to or about anyone – not that any of her neighbours could recall at any rate – and the children she fostered always turned out fine, with nothing but praise and love for their new mum. She'd even received an award on the telly. Gemma thought wistfully of the children this woman had looked after. She imagined coming home from school, opening the front door to be greeted with a kiss and a hug. Gemma smiled. If she closed her eyes, she was almost there.

Hello, Gemma. How was school? Where's my hug then?

'You make me want to puke!' Tarwin roared his anger.

'The feeling is mutual!' Dad raged back.

Gemma's smile vanished as she snapped back to reality. She turned the page.

'I'm going out!' Tarwin yelled.

'No, you're not. You're going to stay at home and do your homework!'

'Like you care whether or not I do my homework!' Tarwin blazed.

'*Roar . . . Ro-aaa-rrr . . . Rooo-aaaa-rrrrr . . .*' Gemma growled to herself like an angry, wounded animal. She didn't bother sticking her fingers in her ears. It did no good – she knew that from experience. But at least she had her scrapbooks.

Gemma turned the page again. Now here was a mum . . . No! She slammed the scrapbook shut and stood up. She was part of this family too. When would Dad and Tarwin realise that? And if the only way to communicate in this house, if the only way to be *visible* was to scream and shout, then she should be there, doing her fair share of the yelling. Gemma headed for the door. Not attempting to disguise her footsteps, she left her room and walked along the landing to the top of the stairs.

Tarwin and her dad stood below in the hall. Tarwin glared up at her, his face contorted with hurt and anger. Gemma's dad glanced at her, then turned away. His gaze was so swift it might never have been. Tarwin had all his attention. A familiar ache began to gnaw at Gemma's stomach.

'Tarwin, I don't understand what's the matter with you.' Dad lowered his voice, trying for a more placatory tone. 'I know we've had our differences but over the last few weeks, you've been impossible.'

'You're what's the matter with me,' Tarwin replied at once. 'Why can't you just leave me alone?'

'You're my son.'

'Like that means anything.'

Gemma took a step down the stairs. She was ignored.

'It means something to me,' Dad tried.

'Tough.'

Gemma walked down another step. No one looked at her. Tarwin and her father stood like two lions in the hall, sizing each other up, circling each other as they tried to get the measure of their opponent. Gemma watched them. They only had eyes for each other. The ache in her stomach was getting worse. It grew in waves, bubbling up inside her, but then, just like that, it faded to nothing. The way it always did. Once again, her moment had passed. Bowing her head, Gemma saw she was still carrying the scrapbook. Her grip on it tightened. Tarwin and Dad might ignore her, but Gemma wasn't totally alone. She had her scrapbooks. She turned and went back to her room.

Once there, Gemma stood on her chair to reach the top of the wardrobe. She didn't want to read this particular scrapbook any more. It had too many happy mums in it. She'd pick one of her other ones – one of her older ones. She hadn't done that in a long time. Gemma pulled a scrapbook out from the bottom of the middle pile on top of her wardrobe. Carefully stepping down, she sat on the soft pile carpet, cross-legged. She opened the scrapbook to the first page.

Oh yes . . . She remembered this one. Most of the mums in this scrapbook didn't have happy tales to tell – to put it mildly. Like this mum. She had four children whom she obviously loved but couldn't take care of – at least, that's what the social services said. There was a picture of the mum with tears in her eyes and spilling over on to her cheeks. Her hair flopped around her tired face. Everything about her face was fatigued. Her lips were turned down, the frown lines on her forehead drooped, even the lines around her eyes sagged. Gemma remembered her as well. She wanted the newspaper to help her get her children back. The paper just wanted the story. The children were fostered and that was the end of that. Gemma never saw the mum in the paper again.

'I'm out of here!' Tarwin no longer roared at Dad, but the icy conviction in his voice made it carry upstairs just the same.

Moments later the front door slammed shut with a force that made the windows in Gemma's bedroom rattle. She glanced up to the top of her wardrobe – she didn't want scrapbooks raining down on her. It was OK. She was safe. Gemma returned to her current scrapbook and turned the page.

2

Mike
Welcome

'I hope you appreciate what we're doing for you,' Gramps said.

Mike didn't answer. What did they expect him to say?

Thank you, Gramps and Nan. Thank you for agreeing to take in your own grandson. Thank you for giving me a home. Yeah, right! Well, thanks for nothing. When Mum and I really needed you, you weren't the slightest bit interested.

Mike lowered his eyes so they wouldn't read what he was thinking on his face. The sun would be the size of a snowball and just as cold before they got a thank you out of him.

'Now then, Robert dear, I'm sure he does appreciate it – as will we.' Nan nodded. 'It will do both of us good to have some young blood in the house again.'

Nan made herself and Gramps sound like a couple of vampires!

'Let's hear the child speak.' Gramps looked straight at Mike. 'Well, boy?'

'My name is Michael, not boy,' Mike snapped. And I'm not a child. But he kept the last defiant statement as a secret, silent thought.

'So you can speak,' Gramps said drily. 'I was beginning to wonder.'

'I can do a lot of things – and you probably won't like any of them,' said Mike.

Gramps and Nan looked at each other. A look that said it all. A look Mike had seen on plenty of other faces over the last year. They had taken one look at him, their guard automatically up, their eyes narrowed with suspicion – and he'd been assessed, judged and sentenced. At his old school, whilst his home life was crumbling into dust, he was known as 'Trouble'. And after . . . afterwards, what was the word his social worker had used to describe him? Uncommunicative. It was funny how the less he spoke, the more nervous some people got.

Mike glared at his grandad. All the long drive down, Mike hadn't said a single, solitary word. He'd nodded, shaken his head or shrugged as appropriate whenever Nan or Gramps asked him a question, but that was it. Mike remembered how months before Gramps and Nan sat together in the courtroom never saying a word to him or each other. And how much he'd hated them for it.

'I know what you're thinking and you needn't worry.' Mike glared at his grandparents. 'I'm not going to disappoint you.'

Let them take that any way they wanted!

'I see that whatever else your mother did, she certainly didn't teach you any manners,' Gramps told him. 'Or respect for your elders.'

'My mum taught me that families are supposed to stick together,' Mike said pointedly.

'Meaning?' Gramps prompted with a frown.

'The meaning can wait until Mike has settled in,' Nan said briskly. 'We're all getting off on the wrong foot here. Come on, Mikey. I'll show you up to your room.'

Nan took hold of one of Mike's smaller bags and led the way up the stairs. Reluctantly, Mike picked up his larger suitcase and followed her. Nan waited until they were on the landing before she spoke again.

'You mustn't mind your grandad,' she said smiling. 'He's all bark and no bite.'

His bark is so bad he doesn't need to bite, Mike couldn't help thinking.

They walked into Mike's new bedroom. Mike stopped short at the sight of it. He looked around, trying not to show how impressed he was. The room was far larger than any bedroom he'd ever been in before. It had cream-coloured walls and a mid-grey carpet. There was a large wardrobe in one corner next to a small, expensive-looking table and chair and there

9

was a double bed against the opposite wall, covered with the thickest duvet Mike had ever seen.

'D'you like it?' Nan asked.

Mike nodded without smiling. Yes, he did like it. So why didn't it make him feel better? If anything, it made him feel worse. When he thought of the holes and hovels he'd been planted in throughout the last year . . . Back and forth, here and there, bounced around like a ping-pong ball. Then there were the places his mum had had to put up with – and was still putting up with. When all the time Nan and Gramps had this huge spare room going begging. Why hadn't they let him and Mum stay in their house before . . . before . . .

'You really do like it, don't you?' Nan asked doubtfully.

'Yes, I do,' Mike forced the words out.

'Good. Your grandad will be pleased.' Nan smiled.

'Why? He doesn't want me here.'

'Nonsense. We both want you here. And you would've been here months ago if your mum had bothered to inform us sooner about what was going on.'

'What does that mean?'

'It means that your mum should've let us know that you were only staying with her friends. You should've been here with us from the start of all this business, but as usual your mother . . .'

'You leave my mum alone.' Mike rounded on Nan at once. 'You don't know the first thing about what Mum and I have gone through.'

After only the slightest pause, Nan replied, 'You're right, of course. I didn't mean to criticise. I can only imagine how tough the last months must've been for both of you. I'm sorry.'

Mike scowled. Suspicious, he searched Nan's face for any sign of insincerity but there was none.

'Will you accept my apology?' Nan asked seriously.

Mike stood still. He didn't answer. But because he didn't say no, Nan took that as a yes.

'I'll give you some time to unpack but don't be too long. Dinner will be ready in half an hour. OK?'

It took several deep breaths before Mike was capable of answering. And even then all he could manage was a nod.

Nan smiled. 'I'm glad you're here, Mike – and so is your grandad.'

And with that she left the room, quietly closing the bedroom door behind her. Mike went over to his bed and sat down heavily. He wondered what his mum was doing now. What was she thinking? Was she thinking about him – and how much she hated him?

3

Gemma
The New Boy

Gemma sat at the back of the class with her bag on the chair next to her. She was reading an article in a tabloid newspaper about another mum. The teacher, Mr Butterworth, entered the classroom. Gemma didn't bother to look up. There was nothing to look up for. She had special powers. She was invisible. Neither Mr Butterworth nor anyone else in the room would even know she was there.

Gemma carefully studied her newspaper article. The mum she was reading about had given herself up to the police a few days after abandoning her son in a shop doorway. Gemma wondered how it must feel to give up your own child like that. What had the mum been thinking as she put her baby down and walked away? What had driven her to do it? And why had she decided to give herself up to the police? Gemma took a long, hard look at the woman. It wasn't a very good photo. The mum was wearing sunglasses and her head was bent and the picture quality was fuzzy – but it *was* a mum. Gemma took a pair of scissors out of her bag and began to cut out the article.

'Settle down, everyone. This is Michael Woods. He's going to be joining our class from today. Who wants to look after him?'

Gemma glanced up. Kane, in front of her, had his hand up. Gemma leaned to one side to see past his back and arm. The new boy – what was his name again? Michael Woods? There he was. Not bad! Tall and slim. Serious looking. Sad eyes . . . It was his eyes that stopped Gemma from returning to her task. *She'd seen those eyes before.* She'd seen this boy before.

But she couldn't have . . . He was new. Gemma frowned as she studied him further. His face was ringing all kinds of bells. If only she could remember . . . The new boy was looking around, his gaze skating across the classroom. Then, suddenly, he was looking straight at Gemma. As they watched each other it was as if the rest of the class had disappeared. Neither of them smiled. Then Mike looked away, his expression never changing.

Surprised, Gemma realised she was holding her breath. She let it out with a hiss and took little sips of air to fill her lungs again. It was OK. She was still invisible. For a moment there, Gemma had been worried that the new boy had seen past her cloak of invisibility. She returned to cutting out her newspaper article.

'Gemma Elliott, what d'you think you're doing?' Mr Butterworth frowned at her.

Gemma looked up.

'Put that away at once.' Mr Butterworth's frown deepened.

Gemma stuffed the newspaper, the article and her scissors back in her bag.

'OK, Michael, sit next to Kane over there. Kane, can you show Michael around at breaktime?'

'Yes, sir.' Kane nodded.

Without a word, Mike made his way across the classroom.

4
Mike
Watching

Mike sat down next to Kane, returning Kane's smile gratefully. Some others in the class were still looking at him but their faces held friendly curiosity. Nothing more. All except the girl behind him. Even now, Mike knew that she was watching him. He could feel her eyes like lasers, boring into his back. He had to fight hard not to turn around and look at her. Did she know his face? *Had she recognised him?*

Come on, Mike. Get a grip! he told himself sternly. He was letting his imagination run riot. No one in London knew him. He was over two hundred miles away from home and there was no way anyone here would find out about him. He had to relax. Life with Gramps and Nan would be difficult enough without him dragging all his worries to school as well. At least at this new school he could remake himself. He wouldn't have to be on the defensive all the time, knowing that others knew about his home circumstances. Being on the defensive was tiring. This was his chance for a fresh start. School was the one place where he could relax and enjoy himself and *be* himself for a change and have some fun.

Mike smiled at his own thoughts. Fun! At school! There had to be something wrong when you longed to go to school and actually thought it was fun! Still, although it was early days yet, this class didn't seem too bad. And Mr Butterworth had been at pains to make him feel at ease as they'd walked along the corridor on their way to the classroom. Maybe things would be all right. Everyone seemed friendly enough – apart from the girl with the probing eyes.

'Kane, who's the girl sitting behind us?' Mike whispered when Mr Butterworth wasn't looking.

Immediately, Kane turned to look. 'Who? Gemma?'

'No! Don't look,' Mike urged, embarrassed. 'You don't have to make it so obvious that we're talking about her.'

Grinning sheepishly, Kane turned to face the front of the classroom.

'Is that her name? Gemma?' Mike asked.

'Yes. Gemma Elliott,' Kane whispered. 'I'd stay away from her though, if I were you.'

'Why?'

'Oh, she's really weird. She doesn't speak much and she stays away from everyone, so everyone stays away from her.'

'Kane, thank you but I'm sure it can wait until breaktime,' Mr Butterworth drawled from the front of the class.

'Sorry, sir,' Kane muttered.

When Mr Butterworth turned back to the board, Mike said softly, 'Sorry. I didn't mean to get you into trouble.'

Kane shrugged and smiled. And Mike knew he had a friend.

5
Gemma
Talking

Gemma glared at Mike and Kane. Their backs were so close she could just reach out and touch them – if she wanted to, which she didn't. Had they been talking about her? What had they said? And that look Kane had given her – like she was there but she wasn't. Everyone looked at her like that. It didn't matter where she was or where she went – home, school or on the street – no one ever saw her. It was the same everywhere. It was as if she was dead. No . . . It was as if she'd never been born. She didn't mean anything to anyone. She didn't make a difference in any way.

But this new boy . . . *He'd* looked at her. What was his name again? Michael Woods . . . There was nothing particularly special about his name. Michael Woods. Mike Woods. Mikey Woods. Spiky Mikey Woods! Gemma grinned at his back. Yeah! That was it. From now on, she'd call him Spiky Mikey!

Without warning, an image flashed in Gemma's head like the blinding flash of a camera. She saw a woman, a *mum*, being pulled away from her son by two policemen. The mum was crying, her face contorted as she screamed her son's name in anguish at being dragged away from him. *Mikey*... The woman had one arm outstretched, her fingers almost touching those of her son. And he was being held back by two policewomen. He was crying too, calling out, reaching out.

The image vanished just as suddenly as it came, leaving Gemma blinking like a stunned owl. Mikey... Michael Woods. *He was in one of her scrapbooks.* Or rather, not just him, but his mum. And if Gemma remembered rightly, his mum was arrested after that picture was taken. But why? Gemma chewed on her bottom lip with frustration as the reason slipped further and further away. It was no use. The image had gone.

Gemma stared at Mike's back in shocked amazement. This boy had been in the newspapers. His mum had been arrested. And if it took her the rest of the week or even the rest of the year, Gemma was going to find out why.

6

Mike
Questions

'OK, how about this one?' Robbie ventured. 'What does a teddy bear grow if he stays awake long enough?'

'I don't know.' Mike smiled. 'What does a teddy bear grow if he stays awake long enough?'

'Tired!'

'Not half as tired as that joke,' Kane groaned.

The other boys around the table laughed. They were eating lunch and already Mike felt settled, like he belonged. The others had made him feel more than welcome.

'Right then. This one will make you laugh. What do you call a bald teddy bear?'

'Oh, come on, Robbie! Give it a rest,' Kane begged.

'Go on. What d'you call a bald teddy bear?'

'I give in,' Kane said, his patience wearing thin.

'Fred Bear! Geddit! Fred Bear . . . threadbare . . .'

Kane picked up a limp lettuce leaf from his plate and threw it at Robbie.

'Er . . . Kane Kingston. I beg your pardon! That's

quite enough of that if you don't mind,' Mr Butterworth called from across the hall.

'Yes, sir,' Kane called back. He turned back to Robbie. 'If I hear one more teddy bear joke I'm going to bring in my little brother's teddy tomorrow and beat you around the head with it!'

'Charming.' Robbie grinned.

Mike smiled and looked around. A girl in the lunch queue across the canteen was watching him. He looked at her and she smiled. He smiled back, then looked away, his face burning. Whoever the girl was, she had to be one of the prettiest Mike had ever seen. She was a black girl with jet hair immaculately plaited back off her head, and the biggest, darkest, most sparkling brown eyes he'd ever seen.

'Who's that girl over there?' Mike asked in what he hoped was a nonchalant, offhand manner.

'Which girl?' Kane asked.

'The one at the front of the queue with the plaits and wearing the blue dress,' said Mike.

Kane turned to have a look, then turned back to Mike with a face-splitting smile. 'That's Robyn Spiner. Why d'you ask?'

'I thought I saw her in our class earlier.' Mike shrugged.

'You did. She sits next to Gennifer – with a "G",' said Kane.

'Oh.' Mike pronged a chip and popped it into his

mouth. When he looked up all the boys at the table were grinning at him.

'What's so funny?' he asked, embarrassed.

'He's in love!' Robbie laughed. 'That didn't take long!'

'Don't talk wet!' Mike muttered. 'I only wondered, that's all.'

'Hello.'

Someone was standing next to him, talking to him. Surprised, Mike looked up from his lunch plate, then stared. It was Gemma. Mike was only too aware that all around his table it had suddenly gone very quiet.

Mike nodded at Gemma, unsure of what to do or say. Why was she singling him out to say hello to in front of everyone? He glanced quickly around the table. He wasn't the only one having that thought.

'Welcome to our school,' Gemma continued.

'Thanks,' Mike mumbled, wishing that she'd go away.

'Have you just moved here then?'

'That's right.'

'Where from?'

'What business is it of yours, Gemma?' Robbie frowned.

'I wasn't talking to you,' Gemma said evenly. She turned back to Mike. 'So where have you just moved here from?'

'Darlington.'

'That's somewhere near Newcastle, isn't it?' Gemma asked.

'Not too far. It's closer to Stockton and Middlesbrough though.'

'That's what I thought,' said Gemma.

Mike's heart was pounding. Beads of sweat prickled through the skin on his forehead. No one spoke. The quieter it got around the table, the louder his blood roared in his ears. Why was she asking all these questions. Did she *know*?

'You don't have much of an accent,' Gemma said thoughtfully.

Mike shrugged. What was he meant to say to that?

'So d'you live with your mum down here then?' asked Gemma.

Around the table, Mike's new friends turned to each other and frowned, wondering what was going on.

'No. I live with my grandparents. I can bring in my full CV and life history tomorrow if you'd like.'

Sniggers erupted at his obvious put-down.

'Just trying to be friendly.' Gemma shrugged. Without another word, she turned and walked away.

'I think you've got an admirer.' Kane raised his eyebrows.

'Gemma!' Robbie snorted. 'You've got to be joking. She's like the bride of Frankenstein!'

Everyone at the table started laughing. Everyone except Mike. He watched Gemma's body stiffen as she walked. Looking round the table Mike wanted to say, 'Shush! She'll hear you,' but how could he? Besides, it was too late. She'd already heard them.

'She can't help it if she's a bit . . . a bit . . .'

'Mousey. Boring. Bizarre. Strange.' Robbie supplied a number of endings to Kane's sentence.

'What's wrong with her exactly?' Mike asked carefully.

'She goes around in a daze.'

'In a world of her own.'

'And she's always cutting up newspapers.'

'Too weird.'

'You said it!'

Comments flew thick and fast around the table.

Mike turned to watch Gemma walk out of the school canteen. He couldn't be sure, but somehow he sensed that she knew she was being talked about. He wondered just what was going on in her head. Something was on her mind, that was for sure. Try as he might, Mike couldn't shake off the feeling of dread falling over him like a shroud. Something told him he hadn't seen the last of Gemma Elliott.

7

Gemma
Searching

very single one of Gemma's scrapbooks were scattered
across the carpet like so many daisies on a lawn. Gemma
cked through first one then another and another, her
impatience growing. She couldn't find what she was
ooking for, but it had to be in one of them.

'Gemma, this is the last time I'm going to call you.
Come for your dinner!' Dad yelled from the hall.

'I don't want any.' Gemma didn't even bother to look
up. She wasn't hungry. She had more important things
on her mind. Like Spiky Mikey!

'Suit yourself!' Dad called back. 'Tarwin, come for
your dinner.'

'I don't want any either!' Gemma heard her brother
call from his room.

'You'll come downstairs and eat it – *now*!' Dad
shouted.

Tarwin's bedroom door opened.

Gemma sighed. 'Here we go!' she muttered to herself.
She wasn't wrong either.

'How come I have to eat my dinner, but prince[ss] madam in her room doesn't?' Tarwin stormed.

'Because I said so. You need to eat,' Dad told hi[m] firmly.

Tarwin needed to eat. She didn't. Gemma pause[d] waiting for the ache in her chest and throat to eas[e]. What was it about Tarwin that had Dad constantly [on] his case? What was it about her that had Dad forev[er] dismissing her? Gemma wished she knew, then may[be] she could do something about it. She couldn't unde[r-] stand it and goodness only knew she'd spent lo[ng] enough trying. Why, she even looked like Dad. Tarw[in] didn't. Tarwin looked like Mum – at least, that's wh[at] he'd told her a while ago.

Gemma wished she could remember something, *any-thing* about her own mum but she couldn't. And because she couldn't, it hurt to try, because she knew she'd fail yet again. She swallowed. Her throat was still hurting. Her saliva felt like shards of glass. She swallowed again. That was better. It didn't hurt so much now.

Tarwin and Dad were still arguing. Gemma let their voices fade away, her mind now fully focused on Michael Woods. She had his picture in one of her scrapbooks, she just knew it. And in that picture he was crying. Not like earlier when he and his friends had been laughing at her.

It was no good. She'd never find anything this way.

She had to do it carefully and methodically or she'd never find the newspaper article. She picked up a scrapbook she'd discarded over an hour ago and opened it to the first page. It was going to take hours to go through all her books, but Gemma was determined. She'd look at every photo and read every headline if she had to.

'I don't know why I bother cooking, I really don't. Right then. As neither of you want your dinner, I'm going to put it in the bin!' Dad called out.

What a big loss that will be! Gemma thought with disdain. What culinary delight was she missing this evening? One of Dad's bean-pot casseroles or another burnt meat offering? She'd pop down once Dad had gone to bed and make herself a cheese or banana sandwich and a glass of orange juice and lemonade. But before then she had some serious work to do.

Gemma turned to the next page.

8

Mike
Your First Day

'How was your first day at school?'

Mike looked at Gramps and Nan, seated at either end of the dinner table. Why couldn't they all sit on the sofa and eat their dinner? Why the formality? Did they eat like this every evening?

'Aren't you going to answer your nan then?' Gramps prompted.

'Sorry, Nan,' Mike replied at once. 'It was OK. I've made some new friends already.'

'Good! Good!'

Mike couldn't fail to see the relieved look which passed between his grandparents.

'I'm not ashamed of anything, even if you are.' Mike's voice was bitter. He hadn't meant to sound so defensive but he knew what was on their minds. They were worried someone might discover who he was.

'We never said you had anything to be ashamed of,' Nan denied.

'But that's what you were thinking,' Mike persisted.

'What's the matter? Are you worried about what the neighbours would say if they knew about your daughter-in-law and your grandson?'

'Mike, don't take that tone with your Nan.' Gramps frowned.

'Michael dear, I'm not thinking about your grandad and me. We're old enough not to care what anyone thinks. It's you I'm worried about,' Nan said gently. 'You try to put on this hard front, like you don't care what anyone thinks, but I know you do.'

'No, I don't.'

If Nan had argued or told him not to be so stupid then Mike would've been OK. But she didn't. Instead she tilted her head to one side and smiled. Just smiled. And that smile put sand in Mike's throat and sent tears from nowhere trickling down his cheeks. Nan sprang up at once. In seconds she had her arm around Mike's shoulders.

'It's all right, love. It's all right,' she soothed. 'You've been through a hell of a lot. Too much really for one boy to stand. I just wish we hadn't had to wait for the court case to hear what was going on.'

'What d'you mean?' Mike sniffed.

He saw Nan look over his head at Gramps, her lips now clamped shut. Gramps shook his head.

'It doesn't matter.' Nan smiled at last. 'What's important is that you're here with us now and we're going to take care of you.'

29

Mike wiped his cheeks with the back of his hand. Taking her cue, Nan went back to her chair.

'I hope you like the dinner we made for you. It's lambsteak pie and mashed potatoes and peas and corn, with fruit jelly or strawberry cheesecake and vanilla ice-cream for pudding. How does that sound?'

'Not bad,' Mike admitted.

Nan started laughing, as did Gramps. And to his surprise, Mike found himself joining in.

They ate in silence for a while, but it wasn't the uneasy silence Mike had been dreading. He looked at Gramps and Nan, smiling at each other between mouthfuls. They were obviously very close, not like his mum and dad over the last few years. And yet Mike could remember a time when his mum and dad had been exactly like this. A time of secret smiles and joking whispers and a lot of laughter between his parents. A time when things were so good, Mike had thought his family couldn't be any happier. But good times never lasted for ever. Mike knew that better than most. Looking at his grandparents, there were so many questions he longed to ask them. And he knew which one was top of his list.

'Why did you never speak to me all the time you were in court?' Mike was halfway through the question before he realised he was speaking out loud, but he didn't stop.

Gramps carefully put down his fork and knife and dabbed at his mouth with his napkin. Delaying tactics.

'We wanted to . . .' Nan began.

'But we were . . . asked not to try and talk to you or communicate in any way,' said Gramps.

'Who asked you?' Mike said, taken aback.

'Your mum's solicitor,' Gramps replied.

Nan rushed on. 'I think your mum felt that with everything else that was going on, it wouldn't be fair to you if we . . . intruded.'

'Intruded?' Mike stared at them, unable to believe what he was hearing. He'd received a couple of smiles from them when they'd all started going to court, but the smiles had soon stopped once the trial got underway. Mike had always thought it was because of all the evidence that came to light. Evidence it was necessary to reveal to try and reduce the charge against Mum. He'd always hated his grandparents for making it so obvious that they were on his dad's side, but now it seemed that perhaps there'd been more to it than that.

'Well, maybe "intrude" is too strong a word.' Gramps looked at Nan. 'But I believe your mum felt it wouldn't be fair to you or us if you were somehow caught between your mum on one side and us on the other.'

'But you're my grandparents.'

Mike would've had to be on another planet to miss the look which passed between Nan and Gramps. They agreed with him. His last argument had obviously been theirs.

'I think in your mum's mind, we were your dad's parents first, the outraged general public second, and being your grandparents came a long way down on the list.' Nan shrugged.

'I see.' Mike's frown lessened only slightly.

That sounded just like his mum trying to protect him again. Protect him from his dad, his grandparents, the media, the whole wide world. It was a shame that the one person she could never protect him from was himself.

9

Gemma
Found

It was in the fourth to last scrapbook. Gemma was beginning to think she'd made a mistake and that she'd never find it, when suddenly, on the last page, there it was. Just as she remembered. Mike and his mum being pulled apart with a huge headline below them which screamed, WIFE OF COMA VICTIM FOUND.

A flash of irritation lanced through Gemma at the lack of details. She'd cut out the headline and the photo as usual and now, for the first time, she found herself desperate to know more about the woman in the picture. Gemma didn't even know her name. She racked her brains to remember more of the story. Snippets flitted tantalisingly before her. Coma victim . . . She remembered something about a house, and a man found in a coma by a neighbour, and a murder trial but that was all. Gemma studied the article closely. Just above the headline she'd caught '14th Ju', but that was all. What was 'Ju'? June or July? Either way it was months ago, almost a year.

Gemma knew which newspaper the headline came from. She recognised its tabloid 'look' so that was no problem. It was definitely from the *Daily Chronicle*, so her first stop after school the next day would be the library. But did they hold newspapers going so far back? Gemma really hoped so.

She turned her attention from Mike's mum to Mike himself. She couldn't resist a secret smile. He'd been laughing at her earlier. Laughing with all his new friends. Well, he certainly wasn't laughing in this picture. Gemma wondered what Kane and the others would say if they saw his picture in her scrapbook. She wondered what Mike would say. He wouldn't be quite so arrogant, that was for sure.

Gemma looked back at Mike's mum. What was she like? What had happened to the man in the coma? Who was he? Gemma wanted to find out about Mike and his mum and all about the events which had led to that picture being taken.

By this time tomorrow, she would.

Mike
Smiles

'What is it with you and Gemma?' Kane asked.

Mike frowned. 'What d'you mean?'

'She's been smiling and nodding in your direction all day.'

So Mike hadn't been imagining it. He wasn't sure if he should feel relieved or even more worried now. It seemed like every time he looked up, she was there with a secret smile on her face. And over the course of the day, it'd got worse. Mike had tried to smile back at first, but Gemma's smile had never wavered, never faltered, never changed. Slowly Mike had realised that Gemma wasn't trying to share a smile with him, she was simply enjoying her own private joke. It was like having someone laugh at you, except that Gemma's smile was far more unsettling, far more sinister. A cat eyeing up a trapped mouse – that was exactly what she reminded him of. She hadn't said a word all day. Not to him or anyone else as far as Mike could tell, and apparently this was a common occurrence. Maybe she was seriously nuts!

It was strange the way she didn't go around with anyone or speak to anyone. She seemed to do her best to fade into the paintwork – except where he was concerned. Maybe his first impressions had been right. Maybe she did know who he was. Maybe... Maybe... Maybe. All these maybes were driving him crazy.

Let it go, he told himself fiercely. He had nothing to be ashamed of. So what if she did know? He didn't care. So what if his heart felt heavy and its thud was almost painful? So what if the queasy, uneasy feeling which had been turning his stomach over all day was growing progressively worse? Mike closed his eyes. Who was he trying to kid? Despite what he told himself, he did care if she knew. He cared very much. And if she did know, what would she do? Wondering about that was the worst thing of all.

11

Gemma
The Library

Gemma sat down in front of the microfiche machine and burst out laughing. At the strange look from the woman next to her, Gemma clamped her lips together, forcing her laugh into an unconvincing cough. She couldn't help it! Every time she thought of Mike, she creased up laughing.

All day, she'd deliberately wound him up by smiling at him. Nothing else. She'd just smiled and watched as he grew more and more uncomfortable. Gemma would never have thought that a smile could be so disconcerting if she hadn't read an article about it in one of her newspapers recently. A psychiatric nurse was being interviewed and she'd said that the patients you never turned your back on were the ones who smiled a lot. Not the ones with happy 'Hello! How are you?' smiles, but the ones whose smiles said, 'I know something you don't . . .' The ones whose smiles said, 'Watch out!' Not that Gemma was mad! Of course not! But her smile had meant that try as he might, Mike hadn't been able to ignore her. At last she'd found someone who couldn't force her to wear her cloak of invisibility.

Pushing Mike's image out of her head, Gemma began to concentrate on the task at hand. She studied the *Daily Chronicle* microfiche backwards, forwards and sideways. There was no story about Mike and his mum on the fourteenth of June. She removed that microfiche and replaced it with the one for the fourteenth of July last year. Page one. Nope. Page two. Nothing. Page three. Nope. Page four. Still nope. Page five.

'Eureka!' Gemma's smile was so broad her facial muscles were beginning to ache. Toning down the unusual outward display of her feelings, she started to read.

Marsha Woods, 44, was arrested last night on a charge of grievous bodily harm. A police spokeswoman told the Daily Chronicle, 'Acting on an anonymous tip-off we apprehended Mrs Woods, who was using her maiden name of Clancy at the time, outside the Saddlers Arms Hotel in Darlington. She had fled from her house with her son, Michael.' Mr Richard Woods, her husband, was found in a coma by a neighbour five nights ago. Marsha Woods is now helping police with their enquiries. It is understood that her son, Michael, is currently staying with friends.

Grievous bodily harm? What had she done? Obviously her husband couldn't have had a heart attack or a stroke if she'd been arrested for GBH. Gemma wondered how much Mike had known about what was going on. Had he known what his mum had done before they'd both gone on the run? Maybe he'd even witnessed it. Mike said he lived with his grandparents. So where was his mum now? Gemma looked at the newspaper picture, at Mike's mum, anguish and fear in every line and curve of her face. Then she thought of Mike, laughing and joking with his friends. His mum deserved someone better than Mike as a child, she really did. Gemma would've been a better child than him. This was so unfair. How come Mike got a mum who obviously cared a great deal about him, whilst Gemma . . . Gemma had no one. She had to find out what had happened to Mrs Woods. Everything else in the world had paled into insignificance in comparison.

'I'll find you, Mrs Woods,' Gemma said quietly.

And she was going to go through every single issue of the *Daily Chronicle* right up to the present date until she did.

12

Mike
Two Words

'Hi, Mike.'

Mike's heart sank. He looked straight ahead at the shoulders of the person before him in the queue. He wasn't going to turn around. Maybe he could pretend he hadn't heard her. He certainly wasn't going to lose his place in the queue. He'd been standing waiting for his lunch for ten minutes already. The queue was moving at an arthritic snail's pace.

'Hi, Mike.' Now she was tapping on his shoulder. No escape then.

'Oh, hello, Gemma.' Mike glanced sideways at his friends who were already grinning. Why couldn't this girl just leave him alone?

'Can I talk to you?' Gemma asked.

'I'm listening.'

'In private.'

Mike didn't move. No way was he going anywhere with her. To tell the truth, she gave him the creeps.

'It's about your mother . . .'

Mike stared. His blood turned to ice crystals in his body, in a fast blast from his head down.

'My . . . what about my mum?' Was that really his voice, so breathless, so *scared*?

Don't panic. He mustn't panic. She didn't know. She *couldn't* know.

'I wanted to talk to you about her,' Gemma persisted.

'There's nothing to talk about.' Eyes. Eyes all around him. Watching. And everyone around was listening. Why didn't they go away? Why couldn't everyone just leave him alone. 'My mum's dead.'

The words were out before Mike knew what was happening. And with those words, his body completely froze. He was aware without having to look that he'd wiped the smiles off his friends' faces. They were no longer sniggering and grinning. Embarrassed sympathy had taken over. But it wasn't their reactions which concerned him at that precise moment. It was Gemma's. A strange stillness had come over her. Her eyes narrowed slowly as if she was looking at something she had just stepped in. She moved forward, her head inclined to one side. Mike instinctively stepped back. Gemma took hold of his arm to stop him moving again. She leaned forward, her lips so close to his ear he could feel her warm, moist breath on his skin. She whispered something to him. Two words.

'Marsha Clancy.'

Just two words. But they were enough to fracture the

ice inside and around him and set his whole body on fire.

Gemma turned and walked away. Mike watched her go. All he could think about was that she knew.

She knew.

13

Gemma
Liar

Liar! How dare he lie about his mum like that? How *dare* he? It had taken Gemma three days of going back to the library each evening and scouring the Daily Chronicle microfiches and other newspapers to find out about Mike's mum. And he was a liar. How could he look her straight in the eyes, open his mouth and lie like that? He was despicable.

And to think she'd wanted to say how very sorry she was about what had happened to his mum. She'd done her best to bury her envy at his ability to make friends, and tried to tell him that she understood about his mum, that she *sympathised*. She knew what it was like not to have a mum. She knew what it did to you. But to deny he had one . . . To tell everyone that his mum was dead . . .

By the time Gemma sat down on her favourite bench in the school grounds, she was shaking. She looked around. There was a game of rounders going on and others were sitting around in groups reading or playing games. Gemma seemed to be the only one who was by herself. Invisible again. She should be used to it by now, but she wasn't. She had been invisible for as long as she could remember. In fact, she couldn't remember being any other way.

That was why, when it got too much to bear, she'd play a secret game and pretend she was wearing a cloak of invisibility. But the truth was, it wasn't a cloak she really wanted to wear, but one that others had forced upon her. And she hated it.

Gemma bent her head. Who was she trying to kid with her secret thoughts of invisibility? She was about as invisible as the bench she was sitting on. And she commanded about as much attention. It wasn't that she was hated – even that would've been better than nothing. But all she got was indifference. At home, at school – the place didn't matter. She was treated the same way wherever she was, wherever she went.

That's why she just couldn't understand Mike.

He had a mum. Why would he want to become like her? He already had the kind of popularity that Gemma could only dream of. What made him want to turn his back on all that? Gemma knew only too well the moment she had started to disappear. It had been when her mum had died years before. And by saying what he had, Mike had declared out loud that he wanted to be just like her. Why? *Why?*

14

Mike
Find Her

He had to find her. Where had she gone? Mike ran down the school corridor, looking in classroom after classroom. With each step he grew more and more desperate. Apart from the girls' toilets – and he certainly wasn't going in there – there was only one place he hadn't tried. Outside. She had to be outside. What would he do if she wasn't?

You mustn't panic, he told himself sternly. Just find her first, then you can sort out everything else.

Mike ran out of the school building and followed the path around to the grounds. He saw her almost at once, sitting on her own. He stopped running, watching her from behind, waiting to get his breath back. Gemma's shoulders were slumped, her head drooped, her whole body was closed in on itself as if she was trying to make it as small as she could.

Funny that she should be the one to know about his mum. How had she found out? Had she always known? No, Mike didn't think so – but that was academic now.

He had to decide what he was going to do. If only he hadn't said that his mum was dead – and not just in front of her, but everyone. Mike still didn't know why he'd said that. Maybe because saying his mum was dead was easier than telling the truth. A wave of self-disgust washed over him. That was what it was all about, wasn't it? That was always what it was about – what was easiest for him.

As if she knew she was being watched, Gemma turned her head. They watched each other as countless moments ticked away. Mike tried for a tentative smile. It was not returned. Instead, the look Gemma cast him was one of pure disgust. As Mike started walking towards her, Gemma turned away. Mike's steps slowed but didn't stop. He walked around the bench to stand before her. She looked up at him, still not speaking. He wished she would say something, anything. After a moment's hesitation, he sat down.

'Hi,' he began. 'I've been looking for you.'

Gemma looked at him. 'Why?'

'I'd like to talk to you.'

'I'm listening.' Gemma turned to stare straight ahead.

'You said . . . Marsha Clancy, before. Just now. In the canteen.' Mike knew he was rambling but he couldn't help it. All at once he was sorry he'd found her. Maybe he should've left well enough alone.

'So?'

'Why did you say that name?' Mike asked.

46

'That's your mum, isn't it?' Gemma was looking straight at him now, her expression fierce.

'Yes, she's my mum.' Mike's voice came out in a whisper.

'Why did you say she was dead?'

Mike hung his head. 'I don't know. It came out before I knew what was happening.'

'It was a wicked thing to say.' Gemma's voice was soft as petals and hard as steel. 'Your mum's not dead. She's in prison.'

And in that moment, the whole world came crashing down around Mike's head. He could hear the sky falling to be followed by a silence like nothing he'd ever known before. He felt sick, like he was actually going to vomit. His mouth kept filling with saliva. He swallowed and swallowed, willing himself not to throw up. He didn't say a word because he couldn't. Gemma didn't speak either. They sat in a bubble of silence. Until Gemma had said those words – 'she's in prison' – there was always hope, the slim chance that she might somehow know his mum's name but not much else. Now that hope had vanished.

'So what're you going to do?' Mike asked at last.

Gemma looked surprised at the question. 'Me? I'm not going to do anything. What d'you want me to do?'

Mike didn't reply.

'Did your mum really . . . really do what the papers said?' Gemma asked.

'She . . . It was an accident,' Mike whispered.

'What happened?'

Mike shrugged. 'Dad liked to . . . play games. Mum and I learnt to be terrified of him and that's the way he liked it. Then one day he went too far and . . .' Mike paused as he waited for his voice to start working again. 'D-Dad fell and hit his head. He was in a coma for ages but then he died and Mum was charged with manslaughter.' The words came out faster and faster, like a dam which had burst its barrier. 'She was trying to protect me. Mum's always trying to protect me.'

'Are you ashamed of her?'

'No, of course not.' The angry denial came out at once. 'My mum . . . my mum's the best mum in the world.'

'You're the one who said she was dead, not me,' Gemma reminded him.

Mike hung his head. No matter how he tried, he just couldn't come up with a way of arguing for what he'd done. Even now he was appalled at the words that had spilt out of his mouth. He wasn't ashamed of his mum. He was ashamed of himself.

'Have you seen your mum since she went to prison?'

'No.'

'But that was over three months ago.'

'I see you've done your homework.' Snatches of contempt fell out alongside Mike's words.

'It wasn't that difficult.' Gemma shrugged.

'Why the interest?' Mike tried to keep his voice even this time.

'I remembered a picture of your mum – and you,' Gemma said. 'Your mum looked . . . nice, so I remembered her.'

Mike frowned. As far as he was aware, the only picture the papers had of his mum and him together was the one taken outside the Saddler's Arms where his mum had been arrested. But that photo was taken months and months ago. Had Gemma recognised him from that photograph? He'd grown a little, lost a lot of weight and he now wore glasses for schoolwork. All those changes and she'd still recognised him? Mike turned to look at Gemma. She was so . . . strange. Try as he might, he just couldn't figure her out.

'Didn't your friends think it strange that you should come charging after me?' asked Gemma.

'I didn't . . .'

Gemma looked at him and the denial died on Mike's lips. No more lies. Instead he shrugged.

'You should've finished your lunch first at least.' Gemma smiled drily.

Mike shrugged again.

Silence.

'So how come you didn't have any lunch?' Mike continued.

'I spent all my money this morning,' Gemma replied.

Mike remembered all the newspapers bulging out of

her bag, the tabloids and broadsheets. Was that where her lunch money had gone?

'I'll . . . I can lend you some money if you like,' Mike said, his face burning.

Gemma turned to look at him, a deep frown cutting into her face.

'For your lunch,' Mike hastened on. 'If you'd like.' Maybe this is the moment where we become friends, he thought.

If only he could tell what Gemma was thinking.

15

Gemma
Lunch Money

Try as she might, Gemma couldn't figure out what Mike was thinking. For one split second she had actually thought he was trying to buy her off. But that was ludicrous. Mike wasn't like that – at least, she didn't think so. And yet . . . Why would he offer to lend her money?

'There are no strings attached. You could pay me back tomorrow – or whenever,' Mike continued.

'Why?'

'Cos I'm not giving you the money.' Mike frowned. 'It's just a loan, that's all.'

'I didn't mean that,' Gemma dismissed. 'I meant why are you lending me the money in the first place?'

'I just thought you'd like some lunch.'

'Oh.' Gemma thought for a moment. 'OK then. I am hungry. I'll pay you back at the beginning of next week.'

'Fine,' Mike said, relieved. He dug into his pocket and took out a number of coins. 'There you are.'

Gemma hesitated, then reached out a reluctant hand

and took the money. 'I'm going to pay you back, OK? Every penny.'

'OK. OK. Let's go and get some lunch.'

They stood up and walked along the path towards the canteen together. Gemma couldn't remember the last time she'd gone for lunch with someone. She looked at Mike. He looked at her.

'I'm sorry about your mum,' she said, for the sake of saying something.

Mike didn't reply.

'My own mum died when I was four.' Gemma's voice was quiet. 'I don't . . . I don't remember what she looked like, to be honest, and Dad doesn't have any pictures of her.'

They carried on walking.

'At least you can see your mum. At least you know that someday you'll be back together.'

Mike still didn't speak.

'How long will she be in prison for?' Gemma hoped he didn't mind her asking. She wasn't being nosy, not really. She was just very interested.

'Mum was sentenced to ten years.'

'Ten years!' Gemma was shocked.

'But her lawyer is trying to lodge an appeal. We're hoping her sentence will be reduced.'

Ten years. The last newspaper article Gemma had seen said that Mike's mum had been found guilty and that sentencing was going to be delayed until the judge had read various social and psychiatric reports. Gemma had no idea Mike's mum had been put in prison for so long. She'd obviously missed the newspaper articles which reported the sentence. From what she had read, it seemed that Mike's mum had hit her husband, knocked him out and left him in a coma before fleeing with Mike. Gemma remembered reading that Marsha Clancy – or Woods, to use her married name – had claimed mental and physical abuse but the judge had been unsympathetic. He'd warned Mike's mum that pending the reports, he was inclined towards a harsher sentence as 'too many women were claiming abuse in circumstances where no abuse could be proven.' Most of the newspapers had been on Mike's mum's side. Some had not.

'So now you live with your grandparents?'

'That's right. I was dreading it at first, but they're not so bad,' Mike said. 'I . . . I blamed them for a while for not coming to help us sooner.'

'But you don't blame them now?'

'To be honest, I don't think they knew what was really happening – not until the trial at any rate. We lived over two hundred miles away so we didn't visit each other that often – especially after Dad lost his job. Besides, Dad was their son. Mum was just their daughter-in-law, so she was hardly going to tell them what was going on inside our house.'

'You mean your grandparents are your dad's family, not your mum's,' Gemma asked, surprised.

Mike nodded. 'Mum's parents both died before I was born.'

They walked in silence as Gemma digested this piece of news. She wondered how she'd feel if she was in Mike's position.

'It must be so hard to live with your grandparents, knowing your mum is in prison for the manslaughter of their son,' Gemma ventured. 'I'm sure I'd feel like I was walking on broken glass all the time. I'd be afraid to do or say the wrong thing in case I upset them.'

'That's exactly how it feels.' Mike stopped to stare at Gemma. 'I feel like I shouldn't be there – because of my mum. But then there's my dad – and he *was* my dad.'

'And here you are stuck in the middle,' said Gemma.

'That's exactly right.'

Mike and Gemma exchanged a smile.

It's going to be all right, Gemma thought, her smile widening. She and Mike had something in common and they understood each other. Maybe they could even be friends. For the first time in a long, long while Gemma found she had something to look forward to. It was such a rare, exciting feeling that Gemma felt it fizzing in her like sherbet. Mike was talking to her, confiding in her. She wasn't invisible any more. She *mattered*.

16

Mike
Stay Put

'So what sort of things were going on in your house?' Gemma asked.

Mike inhaled sharply. Gemma certainly didn't mess about, did she? She looked him in the eye and came right out and asked him. Nobody had ever done that before – not even the social workers and the probation officers. They'd taken ages beating around the bush, trying to ask him exactly that question. At first he'd said nothing, afraid that every syllable might reveal the truth. Then he tried to cover up for both Mum and Dad, but that didn't work either. Like his mum, he didn't believe in airing their dirty family linen for the whole world to see.

How was he supposed to open his mouth and tell strangers about the cruel mental games his dad liked to play on him and his mum? Just thinking about them made his mind turn cold and his blood run boiling hot. How was he supposed to tell strangers that he had plenty of scars, only they were deep inside where they couldn't be seen. It was only when he realised that in trying to protect his mum's privacy and his dad's reputation, he was hurting his mum, that he gave in and told the truth. Only by that time, no one believed what he had to say. He'd left it too late.

'Mike?'

Mike snapped back to the present, aware that Gemma was watching him, waiting for his answer.

Mike shrugged, looking out over the grounds. 'We did OK, unless Dad had been drinking. He was made redundant a while ago and he couldn't find a job, so he started drinking. He was dangerous when he'd been drinking. He hated the whole world then, but he didn't have the whole world in front of him. Just Mum and me. But mainly Mum. Mum protected me.'

'I see. Were you with your mum until . . . until she was sentenced?' Gemma asked.

'No. Once the police caught up with us, Mum was remanded in custody and I stayed with one of Mum's friends. After that I stayed at a foster home for a while, but I hated it. After Mum was sentenced, she said I had to stay with Gramps and Nan. I didn't want to but she wrote to them – and here I am.'

'But you told me they're not too bad,' Gemma said.

'They're OK – in their own way. It's not ideal though. To be honest, it's like living with strangers. I don't really know them. Not well. After Dad was made redundant, we only saw them about once a year, if that. I feel like we're . . . we're worlds apart.'

They reached the canteen and, opening the door, immediately found themselves at the back of the queue.

'What're you going to have?' Gemma asked. 'I didn't get a chance to see what was on offer.'

Mike looked around, nervously. There they were – Kane and Robbie and the others. He could see them. And more importantly, they could see him. They were watching him. They could see him standing next to Gemma. He couldn't join them now – they'd only ask all kinds of questions he didn't want to answer. But he couldn't stay put either.

'I . . . I have to go now,' Mike said quickly. 'Enjoy your lunch.'

Without giving Gemma a second to respond, Mike walked out of the canteen. He didn't have to look back to know that Gemma was watching him.

17

Gemma
Biting

Gemma could feel the coins biting into her hands as she clenched her fists. OK, so Mike couldn't wait to get away from her, but did he have to make it so obvious? A few people around her were staring and sniggering. What was it about her that made everyone run in the opposite direction? Couldn't he have just waited in the queue with her? Was that asking so much? Apparently it was.

Gemma stood stock still, staring after Mike. She watched him until he turned the corner and was out of sight. Slowly, she became aware of the pain in her hands as the coins he'd given her bit deeper into her palms. She longed to go after him and tell him to keep his rotten money. She wanted to throw it back in his face. That's what she should do. She was all right to chat to as long as no one else was watching – was that it? OK in private. Invisible in public.

'Are you going to move up or what?' the boy behind her asked impatiently.

Gemma looked ahead. Quite a gap had opened up in the queue. She looked down at the money in her hands. Lunch money? Friendship money? Or just leave-me-alone money? It was so stupid of her to think it was anything but the latter. Without a word she moved to stand directly behind the person ahead of her. Mike had given her this money to buy herself some lunch, and that was just what she was going to do. If that was the way he wanted it, then fine. Two could play that game.

59

18
Mike
Guilty

Lunchtime was over and everyone was in the classroom.

'Butterworth's late. That's not like him,' Kane said, sitting on top of his table.

Mike didn't dare look in Gemma's direction. Not once. He chatted with Kane and tried not to think of his empty, protesting stomach. What was she doing now? Was she behind him, watching him? Or was she cutting out more newspaper articles?

I wonder why she does that, Mike thought. Maybe . . .

That's enough, he told himself sternly. He was determined not to think about Gemma. She was too complicated. OK, so he'd given her some lunch money and he'd probably said more to her in the last few days than most people at school had said to her in the last few months, and yet here he was feeling guilty. He was going to keep away from Gemma. She was bad news. Aggravation. And aggravation was the one thing he could do without. He'd had enough aggravation over the past year to last him a lifetime and beyond. He was going to spend the rest of his life keeping himself to himself. He wasn't going to get caught up in anyone else's problems but his own. He'd made that promise to himself practically every day since his dad had died.

Mike closed his eyes. Immediately he could see his dad falling, falling, falling in slow motion. Falling so slowly it was as if he'd never hit the ground. Mike opened his eyes at once, forcing the image away.

It took a while.

Funny how after all this time, the image grew steadily more difficult to force out of his mind rather than easier. All he had to do was close his eyes and his dad was back, like a cheap magician's trick. The past was playing in his mind again.

Dad was pushing him, pushing him out of the way and Mike stood there, his fists clenched as he longed to push back.

Mike's fists were clenched now. Slowly, painfully, he straightened out his aching fingers.

If only he could stop feeling guilty all the time. Gemma wasn't his fault. Just as his mother wasn't his fault. She wasn't. *She wasn't* . . .

19

Gemma
The Truth

They sat at the dinner table in the sitting room. Dad sat at the head of the table, with Tarwin and Gemma on either side of him facing each other. They were having dinner together – a rare occurrence – but no one had said a word in almost ten minutes. If the meal wasn't already indigestible, the atmosphere would certainly have made it so.

Gemma's arm was beginning to ache from trying to cut into the overcooked lamb on her plate. At last, a piece gave way. Gemma took a deep breath and popped it in her mouth. It was dry and tough and chewy. Lucky her teeth were all in good condition or she'd be in danger of losing one – or wearing them out at any rate!

'Dad, I've got something to tell you,' Tarwin said suddenly.

Oh-oh! Light the blue touchpaper, then stand well back! Gemma kept her eyes on her plate.

'I've quit school. I've told them that I'm not going back,' Tarwin continued.

Gemma's head snapped up as if it was on elastic. Whatever else she'd been expecting, it hadn't been that.

'You've done *what*?' Dad's knife and fork clattered on to his plate.

'I want to get a job. I want . . . I need my own place,' said Tarwin. His tone was defiant and yet Gemma could've sworn there was more than a hint of unhappiness in it too. Tarwin seemed to be upset about his decision and for the life of her Gemma couldn't figure out why. She turned from Tarwin to her father. Would her dad notice? Not from the look on his face.

'Have you lost your mind? What about your A levels?' Dad stared, astounded.

'When I have a job and my own place, I'll start taking evening classes and study for them that way,' Tarwin recited what was obviously a rehearsed speech.

'No way. I won't allow it.' Mount Vesuvius had nothing on Dad.

'You can't do anything about it.'

'You still live under my roof.'

'Not for much longer,' said Tarwin with satisfaction. 'That's the point.'

'And all this is to get away from me, is it?'

Gemma watched as the hurt he couldn't hide played across her dad's face. So far she hadn't said a word and she wasn't going to either. She and Tarwin had never really had that much to say to each other, but when Tarwin had announced his intention to leave, Gemma's

63

stomach had lurched, leaving her strangely breathless. She didn't want Tarwin to go – and the realisation shook her. Gemma lifted up her napkin to her mouth and used her tongue to push the meat out into it. She rolled up the paper napkin and placed it on her lap. She should say something, she should be involved too, but for the life of her she could think of nothing to say.

'I don't know what's the matter with you these days.' Dad shook his head. 'It doesn't matter what I do or say – it's always wrong.'

'That's just how I feel,' Tarwin said bitterly.

'Tarwin, don't do this. You are about to make the biggest mistake of your life,' Dad said. His voice was terse, as if each word was being tightly reined.

'It wouldn't be the first time someone in this house made a big mistake, would it?' Tarwin replied.

Dad's face drained of all colour. Gemma watched as his Adam's apple bobbed up and down in his throat. He suddenly looked old and lonely and very tired. His skin looked like parchment and his eyes were dull and washed out. At the sight of him, unexpected tears pricked at Gemma's eyes.

'Are you all right, Dad?' Gemma asked. She rounded on her brother. 'See what you've done?'

'Why don't you mind your own business,' Tarwin snapped.

'Don't talk to your sister like that.'

'Why not? You do.'

'Tarwin, you have no right to talk to me like that. You should treat me with respect.'

They were off again.

'I wish Mum were here,' Gemma sighed.

'Mum had too much sense to hang around this dump,' Tarwin said bitterly. 'She took off as soon as she could and I don't blame her.'

Gemma stared at Tarwin. 'What're you talking about? Mum's dead.'

'Course she isn't. That's just what Dad told you to stop you asking for Mum all the time.'

'What?' Gemma's head snapped around to face her father. 'Mum's *alive*?'

'Gemma . . .'

Gemma leapt to her feet. Her eyes blazed with a fiery life neither Tarwin nor her dad had ever seen before.

'Is Mum alive?'

Silence.

Tarwin and Dad looked at each other. Tarwin was the first to glance away. He looked at Gemma, contrite.

'Look, Gem, I shouldn't . . .'

But Gemma didn't want to hear it.

'*Is Mum alive?*' she shouted at her dad.

'Gemma, I . . .' The look on her face froze any words of explanation Dad wanted to say. He nodded slowly. 'Yes.'

Gemma's head was whirling. It was as if she was

standing in a lift many storeys up and it was suddenly plummeting uncontrollably towards the basement.

'Where is she?'

'Gemma . . .'

'*Where is she?*' Her fists banged down on the table making the crockery and cutlery jump.

'I don't know. I really don't – that's the truth,' Dad insisted.

'The truth? You wouldn't know the truth if it rained all over you. All this time, *all these years*, you let me think my mum was dead and she's not. She's out there somewhere and . . . and . . .' And only then did the consequences of what had just been said hit her, really hit her. 'I hate you. I'll never forgive you for lying to me – never.'

'Listen, Gemma . . .' Dad was on his feet now.

But Gemma didn't wait to hear any more. She raced out of the room. She couldn't bear to be anywhere near her dad. He was a liar – and worse.

Somewhere out there, near or far, for better or for worse, her mum was *alive*.

20

Mike
Visiting

Come on, Mike. Ask them. Just open your mouth and ask them. They can only say no. Only.

For the past hour, Mike had been trying to work up the courage to ask something that had been on his mind for a while.

'Gramps? Nan? When can I go to see Mum?'

Grandad and Nan looked at each other.

'I mean, I haven't seen her in months,' Mike rushed on. Now he'd actually asked the question, he was afraid to hear their answer.

'When would you like to see her?' Nan asked carefully.

'As soon as possible,' Mike replied. *Before I start to believe my own lies,* he added silently.

'I'll find out the procedure for prison visits and then we'll all travel up to the prison together.'

'So you'll come with me to see her?' Mike was unable to keep the surprise out of his voice.

'We'll accompany you to the prison. And we'll be there if you need us . . .' Nan began.

'But you can go in and see your mum by yourself,' said Gramps firmly.

'What your grandad means is . . .' began Nan.

'I know exactly what Gramps means,' Mike interrupted.

He turned his head away so they couldn't see his expression. He tried not to mind, he tried his hardest. But he failed. He was disappointed. And more than that, he was hurt.

21

Gemma
Control

Gemma stared out of her window at the night sky. The full moon shone silver at the edge of a cloud. The cloud grew lighter and brighter as it moved in front of the moon. Maybe her mum was looking up at the very same scene at that precise moment.

Somewhere out there was Gemma's mum. She wasn't dead – she was *alive*. All this time Gemma had thought she was invisible because her mum had died, only to find it was all a lie. She'd thought the reason she couldn't seem to make friends or talk to other people was because she lived in this house with no one to talk to, no one to advise her. Dad and Tarwin were totally wrapped up in themselves – and each other. Gemma had always believed that if her mum was still alive . . . And now she'd found out precisely that.

She sat on her bed, her mum's scarf draped over her bedside lamp. She was a fool. The biggest fool in the universe. Everyone lied to her. Or ignored her. She was nothing. She was no one. She was like water running down a plughole. She had no control over anything. And she was so sick of being nothing. Somehow, in some way, she had to make a difference.

Gemma opened her latest scrapbook. She stared at the mum in the photo – a happy, smiling mum hugging her husband. Gemma turned the page. A single drop of water fell on the newspaper article. Slowly, the tiny dome of water flattened as it spread out, soaking into the paper. Gemma slammed the scrapbook shut and threw it against the wall.

'Gemma, can I come in?'

Gemma scooted into her bed, pulling the blankets up to her neck as she turned to lie on her side. She stretched out an arm to turn off the lamp but she was too late, her bedroom door opened.

'Gemma, can I talk to you?'

'I'm sleepy, Dad.'

'It's about your mother.'

'I'm very tired. Can we do this some other time?' Gemma turned her head into her pillow.

She felt the foot of her bed sink as Dad sat down.

'I know I shouldn't have done it. It's just that you were only four and you kept crying and crying for your mum. It seemed to go on forever so I decided . . .'

Gemma sat up to glare at her dad. 'Yes?'

'I decided it would be easier if you thought she was dead. Then you wouldn't break your heart every day thinking she was coming back.'

'It would be easier for who? For you?'

Gemma's dad sighed. 'I wasn't just thinking about myself in all this. I know it doesn't seem like it but I wasn't being totally selfish. You were so unhappy.'

'Unlike the past couple of years when I've been ecstatic.' Gemma wanted to scream and scream at her dad until he realised just what he'd done. 'My mum's out there somewhere and I'm going to find her and . . .'

'And what? Gemma, your mum left us – not the other way around. She didn't want us.'

'She . . . she . . .' The denial dried on Gemma's lips.

'I'm sorry. I shouldn't have said that. There's more to it than that.' Dad shook his head.

'And you really don't know where she is?'

'No. Not any more,' Dad admitted.

'Why has she never been to see us?' Gemma looked up at all the scrapbooks on top of her wardrobe. They lay there, mocking her.

'We moved and she lost touch,' Dad sighed. 'It's very complicated.'

'I'm not stupid. Explain it to me. You can use words of two syllables if you have to.'

Dad looked at her, obviously searching for the right words. 'Gemma, believe me, your mum loved you. It was just that your mum and I . . . well, we couldn't live together any more.'

But his words bounced off Gemma like rainwater off a corrugated iron roof. She heard him, his words echoed in her head but they had no effect. Actions spoke louder than words and the plain fact was, her mum hadn't been to see her. Not once. Not even a Christmas card or a birthday card.

'Did Mum love you?'

'When we first got married. Not when she left,' Dad admitted. 'By then we were better apart than together.'

'Do you still love her?'

Dad looked like he might not answer. But then he spoke. Just one word, whispered softly. 'Yes.'

Gemma looked at her father, really looked at him. It was as if she was seeing him for the first time. Dad. A lonely, bitter, old man. Old before his time but old nonetheless. And it was because of him that her mum had gone away. It was because of him that she had nothing now. Not even an illusion to cling to.

'Goodnight, Dad.' Gemma settled down in her bed, turning away from her father.

'Gemma, I did what I thought was best,' Dad repeated.

'I know.'

'Look, is there anything you want to ask me?'

Gemma turned her head. 'Tarwin's known about Mum all along, hasn't he?'

Dad nodded.

'Is that why you and him are always fighting – because he knew the truth about Mum?'

At first Gemma thought that Dad wasn't going to answer, but then he sighed and nodded.

'Tarwin was . . . Tarwin is very like your mum.' Dad bowed his head.

'And I'm like you,' Gemma finished bitterly. 'That's why Tarwin's your favourite.'

'That's not true,' Dad denied at once.

'Yes it is. For the last couple of years, as far as you were concerned, your only child was Tarwin. It's not as if I came second after Tarwin – I wasn't even in the race. As far as you were concerned, I didn't exist. I was nowhere.'

'What're you talking about?' Dad asked earnestly. 'I'm sorry if you felt I was neglecting you, but I never did. At least, I never meant to. I was just trying to sort things out between me and Tarwin.'

'And what about me?'

'You were doing fine. Your school reports all said you were doing OK.'

'And that's it?' Gemma said scornfully. 'If my school reports say I'm handing in my homework then the rest of my life must be OK?'

'If something was wrong, you would've said . . .'

Gemma stared with disbelief at her dad.

'You don't know a thing about me,' she said with disgust.

'That's not true.' Dad shook his head.

'What's my favourite colour then?' asked Gemma.

Dad stared at her.

'OK, here's an easier one. What's my favourite band?' At Dad's blank look, Gemma continued. 'No? How about this one. What's my favourite flavour of ice-cream? Who's my favourite singer? Who's my best friend?'

'Gemma . . .'

'You can't answer any of them, can you?' Gemma was shouting now. 'Well, for your information, I don't have a best friend. And my favourite flavour of ice-cream is chocolate chip.'

'Gemma, please. Listen to me . . .'

'Dad, could you go now please? I'm very tired. Goodnight.'

Dad's words trailed off at the look on Gemma's face. She held her breath as she waited for him to speak, to protest. Nothing. Moments passed. Gemma listened as her dad walked across the room.

'D'you want me to get you anything?' he asked wearily.

Too little, much too late.

'No.'

'Goodnight, Gemma.'

'Goodnight.'

Gemma waited until she heard the door shut before switching on her lamp. The silhouettes of stars and moonbeams and rainbows all around her room left her cold and empty. Removing the scarf from over her lamp, she opened the bottom drawer in her bedside table and stuffed the scarf at the back of it. Now the room was filled with a cold, yellow light. Gemma looked around. This was how her room was going to look from now on. She got out of bed and picked up each of the scrapbooks left on her floor. Standing on her chair, she placed each scrapbook on top of the piles already on her wardrobe. When at last she'd finished she went back to bed, giving the scrapbooks one last look before she turned off her lamp. She knew it would be a long time before she took any of them down again.

22

Mike
Robyn

'Hi, Mike.'

Mike felt his face grow hot as Robyn Spiner smiled at him. She really was gorgeous. And she was so smart. Apparently she never came below third in any school test. Mike had thought that after the first day she'd never look at him twice and yet here she was standing in front of his desk, talking to him. He felt like bowing down in front of her and calling out, 'I'm not worthy! I'm not worthy!'

'Hi, Robyn. How are you?' Mike hoped his voice sounded normal. Like it was an everyday occurrence for him to chat to the best-looking girl in the class.

'I'm fine. This is for you.' Robyn handed Mike a purple envelope.

Surprised, Mike tore it open at once. He started reading.

'Will you be able to come?'

'Of course. Wouldn't miss it,' Mike replied eagerly. He knew he should check with Nan and Gramps first, but as far as he was concerned that was just academic. An invitation to Robyn's party! Wild horses couldn't keep him away.

'Good. I'm glad.' Robyn walked back to her table.

' "Good. I'm glad." ' Kane mimicked, elbowing Mike in the ribs.

'Are you going?' Mike asked, showing Kane his invitation.

'Yeah, but I had mine flung down on my desk,' Kane replied. 'I didn't get the verbal invitation and the fluttering eyelashes that you got.'

'You're just jealous,' Mike laughed.

'Too right!'

Inside Mike was doing a double-back somersault with a half twist! Now this was more like it. Things were definitely looking up. He was off to see his mum soon, Gramps and Nan were not too bad for oldies, and he was getting on OK at school. And now this. Things were *definitely* looking up.

23

Gemma
Hands Off

'Give us a chip, Robyn,' Beth pleaded.

'Shush! Keep your voice down,' Robyn hissed. 'If Mrs Brewer catches us in here with chips, she'll go ballistic.'

'I'd rather be outside anyway. Why d'you want to stay in this grotty library?' Beth asked.

'Cos it's freezing outside. So much for sunny May! It's perishing and you might have anti-freeze flowing in your veins but I don't!' Robyn told her. 'So, is everyone all set for my party on Saturday?'

'Of course.'

'You bet!'

'Can't wait.'

'Good.' Robyn smiled.

'So who's coming?' asked Livia.

'Everyone,' Robyn said with satisfaction. 'But hands off the new boy – OK? He's mine.'

'Who? Michael?' asked Livia.

'Listen to you. "Who? Michael?" Like you didn't

know who I was talking about,' Robyn scoffed. 'You can't fool me. I've seen you looking him up and down.'

'That was just to see if he was labelled,' Livia laughed.

All around the table guffaws of disbelief sounded.

'I mean it, you lot,' Robyn stated. 'Mike is mine. OK?'

'How come you're going to get the most interesting boy we've had at this school in yonks?' Beth asked.

'Cos it's my party!' Robyn grinned.

'Have you already invited Mike?'

'Yep! And he's coming. I told you – everyone is.'

'You are lucky, having your birthday just after the hunkiest guy in the school arrives,' Livia said.

'It was fate.' Robyn gave a mock sigh.

'Is Gemma coming?' Beth lowered her voice just a fraction.

'You must be joking. When has she ever said more than five words to me at any one time?'

'Besides, she's so gloomy, she'd make it feel more like a funeral party than a birthday party,' Beth announced.

'So you didn't invite her?' said Livia.

'What d'you think?' said Robyn. 'As far as I know, she doesn't know a thing about it.'

'She's weird, isn't she?' Livia mused. 'I don't know what to make of her.'

'Does anyone?' asked Beth.

The others tittered, all agreeing with Beth.

Gemma closed her book and gathered up her belongings. She couldn't bear to hear any more. Piling everything into her bag, she slung it over her shoulder. How was she going to get out of the library without being seen by any of them? She was at the back of the library. They were seated at the table in the next aisle down, so unless she waited for all of them to leave or they all faced the wall as she walked past, there was no way they wouldn't know she had heard every syllable of their conversation. Gemma took a deep breath as she walked out of her aisle.

At Robyn's table, it suddenly went very quiet. Gemma couldn't help it. She knew she shouldn't look. She knew she should just keep walking, but she simply couldn't. She turned her head to look at them and her look became a scowl. Robyn, Beth, Livia and Gillian – they all watched her. And of them all, only Robyn looked embarrassed. Gemma had to get out of there before she drowned in the stillness rippling out from their table. She turned and headed for the door. It was only outside the library as she leaned against the wall panting for air, that Gemma realised she'd been holding her breath.

Gemma walked then ran all the way to the girls' toilets. She shut herself in the cubicle furthest away from the door and sat down on the toilet seat, her head in her hands. The ache in her chest was almost unbearable. Gemma took deep breaths and tried to force herself to calm down, but nothing seemed to work. Robyn and the others – they all thought they were so clever. And they all thought Gemma was nothing, with no feelings to hurt and no sense to understand anything that was going on around her. Even if Gemma hadn't been sitting behind them and listening to every word, did they really think that she'd never get to hear of Robyn's party? Or maybe they just figured that she wouldn't care. Well, she did – very much. Gemma would've gone if Robyn had bothered to invite her. She would give her right arm to go. But she hadn't been asked, and everyone in the class knew it. Even Mike had been invited. That one thought burnt more than any other.

Gemma tilted her head back and closed her eyes. How she wished she had someone to talk with. Someone to help her lessen the pain in her chest. She opened her eyes and stared straight ahead. It was time to stop feeling sorry for herself. It was time to take control. She had no one to talk with – but there was someone to talk to.

Gemma stood up and left the cubicle. She wouldn't waste any more time, nor would she stop to think about what she was doing. She had work to do – and there was nothing and no one who could stop her from doing it.

24

Mike
Control

'Mike, can I talk to you?'

Oh no! What did she want now? Why couldn't this girl leave him alone?

'I'm a bit busy at the moment.'

'It won't take long.'

'Yes, but I'm busy.'

'Mike, are you playing football or are you chatting?' Kane called out with impatience.

'It's important,' Gemma stressed, a restraining hand on Mike's arm.

'Mike . . .?' Kane was about to blow a gasket.

'OK! Just a moment!' Mike shouted out. He threw the ball towards Kane before turning back to Gemma. He wasn't sure who he was shouting at – Kane or Gemma. 'What is it?'

'You got an invite to Robyn's party on Saturday?'

'Yes. So? Are you going?'

'No, I'm not,' Gemma replied. 'I'm busy on Saturday.' Why was she asking him about the party? Mike waited for Gemma to continue. She looked down at her feet and around the school grounds and at the school building. Slowly, as he watched her, everything else faded away. Mike knew something was coming, something he wouldn't like.

'It sounds like it'll be a great party,' Mike ventured.

He spoke to fill the silence. He spoke to stop Gemma from speaking. He didn't like the way she was looking at him – like she hated him. What had he done?

'Anyway, I'd better get back to the game.' Mike turned to run back to join his friends.

'I don't want you to go.'

Turning around, Mike frowned deeply. 'Kane's waiting for me. I'm in goal.'

Gemma took a deep breath. 'I don't think you should go – to Robyn's party.'

'Why not?'

Silence.

'Why not?' Mike asked again.

'Your mum's in prison,' Gemma replied softly. 'I don't think Robyn would want a jailbird's son in her house.'

Mike froze. One puff of wind, one whispering breeze and his whole body would shatter into a million, trillion pieces.

'I don't want to tell Robyn about your mum but I will – if you force me to. Tell her this afternoon that you can't go to her party, or I'll tell her why she should take back her invite.'

The silence that stretched between them was bigger than the Grand Canyon. Mike struggled for something to say but his mind was a total blank. He couldn't think, couldn't feel. He kept trying to tell himself that he'd misheard, that somehow he was mistaken and Gemma hadn't warned him off from going to Robyn's party. But he knew from the hard expression on her face that he'd heard every word correctly.

'Tell her you can't go,' Gemma repeated.

She turned and walked away, leaving Mike staring after her.

25

Gemma
I Can't Come

'Er . . . Robyn. Thanks for the invite to your party, but I've just remembered . . .'

Gemma bent under her table to get her bag.

'I can't come. I have to go somewhere on Saturday with my nan and grandad,' Mike continued. 'Sorry. I completely forgot.'

'You can't come?' Robyn said, dismayed. 'But I was hoping you'd be there.'

'Sorry,' Mike mumbled.

'Where're you going on Saturday?' asked Robyn, disappointment written all over her face.

'Out. Gramps and Nan are taking me . . . taking me . . . out,' Mike finished weakly.

'I only have one birthday a year. Can't you ask them to take you out some other time?'

'Believe me, I really wish I could,' Mike replied, his voice shaking slightly. 'But I can't.'

Gemma retrieved her bag and sat back down in her chair. Mike was looking directly at her. Not at Robyn

– at *her*. Gemma felt a slow, burning flush creep over her face and down her body. She wasn't going to be the first one to look away. She wasn't. And she wasn't going to feel guilty either. The sick, gnawing ache in her stomach would soon pass. And if she wiped her hands on her skirt enough times, her palms would stop feeling clammy. And the horrible clawing voice in her head telling her that what she was doing was oh-so wrong would melt away if she ignored it for long enough.

She was helping Mike really, only he was too stupid to realise it. What would happen if Robyn and Kane and the others found out about him and his mum? He didn't want that. Neither did Gemma.

You're not doing this because you're jealous, she told herself. That wasn't it at all, no matter what the voice in her head said. She had Mike's best interests at heart. He'd thank her one day.

Not now.

But one day.

26

Mike
Home

Mike walked home, his head bowed, deep in thought. He was going dizzy trying, but for the life of him he just couldn't figure out what was going on. Why was Gemma so dead against him going to Robyn's party? She'd said Robyn wouldn't want a – what was the phrase she'd used? – a jailbird's son in her house. Jailbird . . . Stupid word. Hateful, stupid word. But only Gemma knew about his mum. If she didn't tell anyone, then no one else would know. Why was she so insistent that if he didn't back out, she'd tell everyone about his mum? And worse than that, why had he given in and done it? Gemma had told him not to go to the party and without a single word of argument, he'd done as he was told. What was the matter with him? So what if Robyn found out? So what if the whole school found out?

Mike's steps slowed. Who was he trying to kid? He would hate it if anyone found out about him and his mum. And just admitting that to himself made him feel like the lowest of the low. Mum had done nothing wrong. Neither he nor his mum had anything to be ashamed of.

Then why is your mum in prison and why are you living with your grandparents?

The thought pushed its way into his head before he could stop it. Mike clenched his fists as he sought to drive it out again. He told himself over and over, 'Mum's done nothing wrong. Mum's done nothing wrong.'

But each time he murmured the words, he felt worse. He turned into the street where he now lived. He glanced down at his watch. He was late. Gramps and Nan expected him back home over an hour ago. What excuse could he come up with?

'I stayed behind at school to volunteer for the school play.'

'I stayed behind to practise for the inter-schools gymnastics competition.'

Or the truth.

'I sat on a bench in the park, trying to sort out my life. I sat and thought until my head was ringing and my mind was spinning and I'd got a raging headache, and it got me precisely nowhere.'

Mike wondered what they'd make of the truth. He wondered what the whole world would make of the truth, the whole truth and nothing but the truth. All he knew was that the truth was eating away at him like a strong acid and he wasn't sure how much more he could take. Mum was in prison – and it was all his fault. With each day that passed, that fact grew harder and harder to bear.

He was a coward when it came to his mum and he was just as much a coward when it came to Gemma. A first-class, grade-A, spineless coward.

27

Gemma
Getting Away

Gemma knocked twice before opening her brother's bedroom door. He was sitting at his table busily writing something on a piece of paper. The moment his door opened, he immediately turned over the piece of paper, his hands moving to cover it protectively.

'Tarwin, can I talk to you?' Gemma hovered in the doorway, waiting for her brother's answer.

'What's the matter?' Tarwin asked.

Gemma took this as an invitation to come further into his bedroom. She closed the door carefully behind her. She looked around. It'd been a long time since she'd last been in his room. It hadn't changed much. Clothes scattered in all four corners. A paper plate of something which looked like it might once have been pizza. A double bed covered with books, superhero comics and magazines. Only the walls were different. All the posters had been taken down. Gemma stared. She couldn't remember ever seeing Tarwin's bedroom walls without posters all over them. Posters of fast bikes, fast cars, fast planes, fast rockets.

'Why did you take your posters down?' Gemma asked.

Tarwin shrugged. 'I'm too old for that sort of thing now.'

'You're only seventeen.'

'I'll be eighteen in a few months.'

Gemma nodded and looked around again. Without the posters, Tarwin's room looked strangely empty. She hadn't really thought about it before now, but maybe Tarwin's posters served the same purpose as her scrapbooks. Maybe whenever things got too tough, Tarwin could just think himself into his posters and off he went in a hurry. She wondered if Tarwin ever dreamt of anything else but getting away.

'So what d'you want?' Tarwin's tone was curt.

'D'you know where Mum is?'

Tarwin put down his pen and swivelled his chair around.

'No, I don't. I wish I did.'

Gemma looked around, kicking idly at the carpet. She was unwilling to leave it there. 'Why didn't you tell me that Mum wasn't . . . wasn't dead?'

Tarwin sighed. 'I wanted to, many times. But Dad said it should come from him – and for once I agreed with him. I really wish you hadn't found out the truth the way you did. I shouldn't have blurted it out like that. It was bang out of order.'

'You should have told me a lot sooner. I know we haven't had much to say to each other recently but you shouldn't have waited for Dad to tell me. In your shoes I would've told you.'

'Would you? Would you really?'

'Yes, of course.'

'I doubt it.' Tarwin's smile was almost sad. 'Gemma, one day you'll find out that life isn't about cutting out the bits you like and want to keep and ignoring all the other bits as if they don't exist. It's more complicated than that.'

Gemma blushed at the thought that Tarwin knew about her . . . her hobby.

'Don't be patronising. I know that.' Gemma scowled.

'Sometimes I wonder if you do.'

Gemma's eyes narrowed suspiciously. 'Have you been looking in my scrapbooks?'

Tarwin looked away, unable to meet Gemma's eyes. It was only momentary, but it was enough.

'You had no right to go through my private stuff. You'd go ballistic if I did that to you!' Gemma stormed.

'Well, you must admit it's a pretty strange thing to do – cutting out photos of different women. It's not like you know any of them.'

'That's not the point. And it's not strange,' Gemma denied. 'You collect comics, I just collect stories.'

Tarwin shrugged. 'If you say so.'

Gemma glared at Tarwin. He started grinning. Desperate to change the subject, she looked from Tarwin to the table behind him. 'What were you so busy writing when I came in?'

Immediately Tarwin turned back, defensively covering the piece of paper with one hand. 'None of your business.'

Gemma stared at her brother. He looked sheepish, almost embarrassed. That could only mean one thing.

'Have you got a girlfriend?' Gemma guessed.

'No . . . of course not . . . no, I . . . don't talk rubbish . . .' Tarwin stumbled over his denial, his face turning beetroot.

'You do!' Gemma smiled. 'I thought so. For the last couple of months you've reeked of aftershave, and that anti-spot cream isn't Dad's and it certainly isn't mine.'

'Well, so what if I do.'

'You've got a girlfriend. I can't believe it. What's she like?'

'She's . . . she's . . .' Tarwin's expression hardened. 'She's none of your business.'

'I only asked. No need to bite my head off. What's her name?'

'Monique. And that's all I'm going to tell you.'

'Oh, for goodness sake! I only wanted to . . . to . . .' Gemma stopped abruptly. She only wanted to what? To get to know her brother. Gemma realised in that moment that the accusation she'd flung at her dad, that he knew nothing about her, applied here too. She knew absolutely nothing about Tarwin either.

'So where did you meet Monique then?'

'At a party. Next question?'

'How come you've never brought her here?' At Tarwin's raised eyebrows, Gemma had to smile. 'You're right, it was a stupid question. So are you two a serious item then, or what?'

Tarwin immediately became watchful. 'I'd say so – yes.'

A sudden thought occurred to Gemma. 'Is that why you're in such a hurry to get a job and a place of your own, so that you two can be together?'

One look at Tarwin's expression of stunned amazement and Gemma had her answer. She said, 'Oh, I get it now. Is Monique going to leave school too?'

'She was, but not any more,' Tarwin answered carefully.

'Are you still going to leave school?'

'I don't know. I'm still thinking about it, but there's no rush now.' Tarwin shrugged.

And that was when the penny dropped, and then some!

'Was there a rush before?' asked Gemma, nonchalantly.

Tarwin's lips immediately clamped together.

'Was she pregnant?' said Gemma.

At first, Gemma thought that Tarwin wasn't going to answer. 'For a while we thought she might be, but then it turned out that she wasn't.'

Silence. Gemma looked at her brother, unsure of what to say. 'I bet that was a relief.'

'No. It wasn't actually,' Tarwin said quietly. 'Not for me anyway.'

'I'm sorry. It's a shame. I would've enjoyed being an auntie.' Gemma smiled. Tarwin smiled back. This was the first real conversation Gemma could remember having with her brother in a long, long time – and she was loving it! 'So am I going to get to meet her?'

'One day,' Tarwin said vaguely.

'Maybe we could all go out for a meal somewhere,' Gemma suggested.

'You expect me to drag around with a little kid like you? Are you nuts?' Tarwin scoffed.

Gemma glared at him. 'Thanks a lot. What does this Monique see in you anyway? Desperate, is she? Or don't her eyes work?'

Tarwin stood up. 'Gemma, get lost.'

Don't spoil it, Gemma. Stop being stupid. Shut up.

But her mouth was ignoring the messages sent from her brain. 'It won't be long now!'

'What won't be long now?' Tarwin frowned.

'Until Monique realises what a fool she's making of herself by going out with a total loser like you. And then she'll dump you so fast, you'll develop a permanent pear shape!' Gemma forced a laugh.

Tarwin took a step forward. Gemma took a step back.

'Out! Now!' Tarwin bellowed.

Gemma ran from the room. Her smile vanished as she closed the bedroom door. What was it about her? Why was it that every time she wanted to talk to someone, to try to get close to someone, all she had to do was open her mouth to push them away? Why was it that every time she opened her mouth, something stupid fell out? Couldn't she do anything but lash out?

Gemma turned and opened her brother's door again. 'Sorry, Tarwin. I didn't mean it. I was just being mean.'

Tarwin didn't bother to turn around. He carried on writing. 'Gemma, I said get lost.'

'I said sorry,' Gemma tried. 'And I won't tell anyone – I promise.'

Tarwin turned, his expression cold as ice. 'And I said, don't slam the door on your way out.'

Gemma left, shutting the door quietly as directed. She leaned against it, wondering as she so often wondered, just what was the matter with her.

28

Mike
Dreaming

Shouting. Mike's father was shouting. His face was contorted with rage. Mike saw his dad clench his fists. He knew what was going to happen next. Mike stepped forward, his arms outstretched. And then, without warning, all the fireworks in the house went off and Mike could do nothing but watch the rockets fly around. He'd duck and jump and dive for cover but the rockets were everywhere. Then a rocket was heading straight for him, and Mike knew he had no time to get out of the way. It was going to hit him and *explode.*

Terrified, he sat bolt upright in his darkened room. Sweat trickled down into his eyes. He wiped his forehead and waited for his lungs to fill with air. He didn't bother to cross the room and switch on his light. There was no point. Besides, Nan had ears like a bat. If he switched on the light, she was sure to hear it and she'd be in his room before he could even get back in bed, asking him if everything was all right. As if anything could ever be all right again.

Mike lay back down and stared into the dark. His thoughts turned to his mum. He wondered what she was doing. Was she asleep or awake? Was she thinking of him or his dad?

And after what Mike had done to her, who did she hate the most? With a faint groan, Mike turned to lie on his side.

'I'm sorry, Mum. I'm so sorry.' He mouthed the words into the darkness.

His life was all secrets. And lies. But he wasn't paying for the lies, his mum was. And the worst thing of all was that Mike was letting her.

29

Gemma
Saturday Night

Gemma was alone in the house. Dad was out. So was Tarwin. She should've been glad. She should've been ecstatic. She had the whole house to herself. But Gemma felt like a pea rattling around all by itself in a tin can. Again and again she found herself thinking of Robyn and her party. They were all there now – the rest of her class – having the time of their lives. Great music, excellent food and non-stop laughter. Gemma just had to close her eyes to be there. But when she opened her eyes, she was always back in her own dark, dismal house by herself. The silence around her seemed to be mocking her. It was horrible.

When at last she could stand it no longer, Gemma grabbed her coat and slammed out of the house. It was only when she got to her gate that she slowed down.

She had nowhere to go.

Gemma fished her front door keys out of her pocket. Turning slowly, she went back indoors. The whole class was at Robyn's house. Everyone except her – and Mike.

And if she hadn't said anything, Mike would've been there with the rest of them. He'd been at school for five minutes and he belonged. Robyn wanted him at her party. Nobody wanted Gemma. She pulled off her jacket and hung it back up on the peg.

At least two of them in the class weren't at Robyn's party – the most popular boy in the class and the least popular girl. There! She and Mike had something in common after all. They both had popular in their titles.

The more she thought about Mike, the more her insides twisted into knots. It wasn't right. It wasn't *fair*. Why was he so popular? Why was she so despised? She hadn't said anything or done anything to deserve the way they were all treating her. It was all Mike's fault. As the new boy, he could've stood up for her if he'd wanted to. He'd spoken to her about his mum – he hadn't done that with anyone else. Why had he confided in her if she couldn't be trusted? Why had he told her about his feelings if Gemma was nothing? If Mike was worth inviting to a party, why wasn't she?

Well, he wasn't at the party and it was because of her. At least as far as Mike was concerned, Gemma wasn't invisible. And she was going to make sure it stayed that way.

30

Mike
Not That Much

The moment the lunchtime buzzer sounded, the whole class sprang up. An eruption of chatter and laughter filled the room, as did the sound of chairs being scraped across the floor and heavy bags being banged down on tables.

'Er . . . *Did I say I'd finished*?' Butterworth yelled above the noise.

The class quietened down.

'Thank you so much,' Mr Butterworth said with sarcasm. 'I forgot to give you your homework.'

At the collective groan that went up, Mr Butterworth smiled. 'Yes, I know. And if you don't do it, it'll hurt you a lot more than it will hurt me. Exercises forty-seven and forty-eight in your workbooks – and no excuses.'

Mr Butterworth left the classroom first, followed by everyone else. The noise emptied out of the room like water pouring out of a bottle.

'Mike, can I borrow five pounds?'

The words were said so softly, Mike almost thought

he'd imagined them. He turned his head. Gemma was there behind him, watching him intently. They were the last two. Everyone else was heading out of the door.

'Pardon?'

'Can I borrow . . . can I have five pounds please?'

'You haven't given me back the money I lent you last week yet,' Mike reminded her.

'I haven't got it. That's why I'd like to borrow some more. I know you can afford it. Five pounds isn't that much.'

Mike glanced down. He half expected to see subtitles winding their way across the floor telling him just what was going on. There was something bizarre happening. Something written on Gemma's face plain enough for him to read, only for some reason he couldn't quite manage to do so.

'What d'you want it for?' Mike asked.

'I haven't decided yet,' Gemma told him.

Mike frowned at her. What on earth . . .? Then all the cogs in his mind slotted into place and started moving as one. He understood.

'I haven't got five pounds,' he said, still unwilling to believe the evidence of his own ears and eyes.

'Yes, you have,' Gemma argued. 'You, Kane and Patrick are going to the pictures tonight. I heard you talking about it. I'm not taking all your money. I just want five pounds. I need it.'

Mike's body stiffened. 'You're not getting it from me.'

Looking into his eyes, Gemma asked, 'I wonder how Kane and Patrick would feel knowing that their new best friend's mum is in prison. She's in there for manslaughter, but you and I know the truth about you, don't we, Mike? We know why you *really* don't want anyone to know.'

The room started spinning like a gyroscope, up and down and round and round until Mike thought he was going to tumble off the end of the world. And the edges of the world around him were getting darker and darker, like a kaleidoscope closing. In that moment, Mike realised that if he didn't do something – and fast – he was going to pass out. He *couldn't* pass out. Not here. Not now. Not in front of *her*. He closed his eyes briefly to take a concentrated deep breath. When he opened them again, she was still there.

'I wonder how everyone in the class – no, everyone in the whole school – would feel if they knew the truth?' Gemma continued.

'And you'd tell them.' Mike didn't know if it was a statement or a question. His answer was a smile. One of Gemma's secret smiles.

'It is such a shame about your mum.' Gemma shook her head. 'I don't think everyone would understand the way I do.'

The swimming, giddy feeling inside Mike faded. It was making way for something else, something far more powerful. Mike stood in front of Gemma, his fists clenched, his eyes like stones as he looked at her. Without a word, he took five pounds out of his trouser pocket and held it out towards her. Gemma took it without touching him, without looking at it.

'Thanks,' she said.

Moments later she was out of the room and gone.

31

Gemma
Money

Gemma wondered if she'd ever stop throwing up. And it wasn't just her stomach that felt sick. Every cell in her body was revolted by what she'd just done.

After flushing the toilet, Gemma put down the toilet lid and sat down. She was in the end cubicle in the girls' toilets and she never wanted to come out. What had she done? She wiped the back of her hand across her mouth. Only then did she realise she was still holding Mike's money.

It wasn't hers. It would never be hers. She didn't want it. Gemma threw it against the cubicle door. It bounced back at her, falling at her feet. Gemma stared at it, hating it. All night she'd lain awake thinking about her family and comparing it to Mike's. He had a mum who loved him. She didn't. He had grandparents who took him in when he had nowhere else to go. If Gemma had nowhere else to go, who would take her in? Mike had friends. She didn't. He belonged already. She never had. She'd spent the whole night thinking about him and if she was truthful, being jealous. Even though his mum was in prison, he had everything she didn't. So this morning she'd been determined to get something of his. But now she had, she'd never felt so wretched. OK, so she'd asked . . . *told* Mike not to go to Robyn's party, but that was just . . . That was different. Yes, it was horribly spiteful but compared to this . . .

She tried to remember everything she'd said, word for word. Maybe it hadn't come across as taking his money off him in return for keeping quiet. But even as she thought it, Gemma knew she was deluding herself. It had come across as that all right because that's exactly how she'd wanted it to come across. And all that stuff about knowing the truth – that had all come out on the spur of the moment. Instinctively, Gemma had been aware that Mike didn't want anyone to know his mum was in prison. It didn't matter what she was in there for, it could've been for one day or ten years, it was all the same to Mike as far as making it public was concerned. He just didn't want anyone to know. The truth was he was so ashamed of her, he'd rather she was dead than in prison. Gemma had read that much on his face when he'd talked about his mum.

Gemma picked up the five pound note at one corner. She could hardly bear to touch it. She must've been crazy. She'd go and find Mike and give it back and apologise like she never had before.

Gemma left the girls' toilets, gingerly clutching the money. She had to find Mike fast before she lost her nerve. She had to find him before he told anyone what she'd done.

32

Mike
Corners

Mike finally found what he was looking for. A place to be alone. A place to hide. It was right at the back of the library, in the reference section. There was just a single table and no one was sitting at it.

Mike sat down carefully in a chair with his back to the rest of the library. He placed his bag on the floor beside him, wincing as it made a slight sound against the wooden floor. Covering his face with his hands, he forced himself to think. He should tell a teacher or Gramps and Nan. He had to tell someone what was going on. He couldn't allow Gemma to get away with it. How many others in the class was she getting money from? Was that why no one spoke to her? Someone should've warned him.

Mike heard footsteps coming his way. Quickly, he removed his hands from his face. He leaned back in his chair and took the first book off the shelf that his fingers touched. The footsteps turned the corner. Mike glanced up.

Gemma.

Mike scowled as she approached him. What did she want? More money? Cos if she did, she was out of luck. He'd . . . he'd . . . Well, he didn't know what he'd do, but he wouldn't let her take more money from him, that was for sure. Why couldn't she leave him alone? Wasn't he even safe in the library for goodness' sake?

'This is yours.' Gemma held out his five pound note.

Mike looked from it to her. What was she up to?

'Go on. Take it. It's your money,' Gemma insisted.

'I don't know what your game is, but I'm not playing. Now go away. And don't come anywhere near me again.' Mike's voice was low and even. He made a great show of turning in his chair to read the book he had in his hands. He had no idea how he could sound so cool and calm when inside all he wanted to do was . . . was smash things. Smash her.

'I don't want your money,' Gemma said from behind him.

'D'you think I'd take it back – or even touch it after you'd had it?' Mike said, scornfully. 'You want it so badly? You stuff it!'

Silence.

Mike turned his head to see what she was doing – he couldn't help it. Gemma put the five pound note down on the table in front of him. Before Mike was even aware of what he was doing, he picked up the money, scrunching it in his hand in the process, and threw it at her. It hit Gemma in the face, on her cheek, before falling to the floor. They were both outside and beyond time. There was nothing and no one in the universe but them – and the line that had been drawn between them.

'Go on. Take your money,' Mike hissed. 'And I hope it chokes you.'

Gemma bent down. Her fingers curled around the five pound note. She straightened up and walked away without a backwards glance.

Mike put down the book he was holding. He still had no idea what it was and he didn't care. He laid his head on his folded arms resting on the table. He was tired. Tired of the day, the month, the whole year. And he missed his mum so very, very much.

33
Gemma
Moon And Stars

Gemma walked home. The traffic roared past her, people hurried by and usually Gemma scarcely knew they were there. She was always too deep into her own thoughts. But not today. Today she didn't want to think, so she studied every car, every building, every expression on each passing face. She studied and analysed them to stop her mind moving on to other things. She looked into the small newsagent-cum-post-office – the queue was almost at the door. She looked into the baker's shop, watching as a man asked if the doughnuts were fresh.

And then she saw it in the next shop – a boutique. On display in the window was the most beautiful jumper Gemma had ever seen. It was a deep, midnight blue, embroidered with a silver crescent moon and tiny golden stars and moonbeams. Gemma had never seen anything like it before. She looked up to see the name of the shop. *Material Girl*. Why did that name ring a bell? Hang on! Wasn't this Robyn's mum's shop? Yes, it was. Gemma knew she recognised the name. She looked through the window to make sure that Robyn wasn't in there, then she walked in.

'Hi. Can I help you?' a shop assistant asked with a friendly smile.

'Yes, you can. That jumper in the window . . .'

'From the Shayne Jarvis night-time collection?'

Gemma nodded, although she had no idea whether it was or not. 'Yes, that's it. How much is it?'

The shop assistant's smile broadened. 'We've had a lot of interest in those. They're selling like hot cakes. What size were you after?'

'Size ten.'

'Let's see.' The assistant beckoned for Gemma to follow her.

Wending their way past racks of gorgeous skirts, shirts and trousers, the assistant stopped in front of a carousel rack of assorted jumpers. Spinning the carousel around she searched amongst them for Gemma's size.

'Here we are! There are two size tens left. Would you like to try it on?'

Gemma glanced down at her watch. If she tried on the jumper she'd be late home.

'Very quickly then,' Gemma said at last.

The shop assistant showed Gemma to the fitting rooms and handed her the jumper. Gemma pulled off her jacket and burgundy cardigan and pulled the new one over her head. When she looked in the mirror, her mouth fell open. It looked wonderful. *She* looked wonderful. And it fitted like a glove – as if it'd been made just for her. She turned this way and that, looking at her reflection in the mirror. The jumper was amazing. It made *her* look amazing – like a different person. Gemma hardly recognised herself. The colours suited her exactly. She had to have it. Reluctantly, Gemma pulled it off, before looking for the price label. There wasn't one. Putting on her own cardigan and jacket, she left the fitting room.

'So what did you think?' The shop assistant asked.

'It's lovely,' said Gemma. 'How much is it?'

'Forty-nine pounds, ninety-nine.'

Gemma stared. Fifty pounds for a jumper?

'It may sound like a lot but the moon is hand-sewn and the stars and moonbeams are hand-embroidered. These jumpers really are a work of art.'

Gemma looked at the jumper again. She longed to have it but no way could she afford to spend fifty pounds on a jumper. She handed it back.

'Shall I wrap it up for you?'

'Er . . . no, thank you. I can't afford it,' Gemma mumbled.

The shop assistant smiled. 'Maybe you could get your mum and dad to buy it for you for your birthday.'

'Maybe.'

'I'd hurry though. We've only got two more in your size and after that we might not get any more in.'

Gemma nodded, leaving the shop. She turned to take another look at the jumper in the shop window. *Her* jumper. That's how she thought of it now. Could she ask Dad for the money? No way. He'd never give her fifty pounds in one go, and certainly not for a jumper. She might as well ask for the moon. Maybe if she told Dad it was for a school trip...? But what would happen when the trip didn't materialise?

That jumper was going to be hers – she was determined.

With that jumper she could force off her cloak of invisibility for good. With that jumper everyone would notice her, not only Mike. With that jumper she'd be a new person – someone who could look in a mirror without flinching. Gemma had to come up with a way – and fast – of making enough money to buy it. But how? Where on earth was she going to get fifty pounds?

34
Mike
Happy Now

Mike pushed his cabbage and spring greens round and round his plate with his fork. There was a strange silence at the dinner table, each person deep in their own thoughts.

Go on! Ask! Mike thought sternly. Just open your mouth and ask!

'Gramps, when are we going to see Mum? You said we could go and see her soon,' Mike reminded his grandad.

Gramps and Nan exchanged a look.

'I . . . er . . . I've been finding out about it.' Gramps was flustered for some reason. 'Apparently I have to write to . . . to your mother and ask her to send us a visiting order. They won't let us into the prison to see her without one.'

'Haven't you written to her yet?' Mike asked, dismayed.

'No. I haven't got round to it. I'll do it sometime this week.' Gramps nodded.

Sometime this week! Mike couldn't believe it. Gramps was talking about it as if it had the same priority as pruning his roses or hanging a picture on the wall. Didn't he know how much this meant to Mike? Couldn't Gramps see how much Mike needed to see his mum? How could he be so casual about it?

'I want to see my mum,' Mike told him, barely able to contain his rising fury. 'You should've written to her ages ago. I know you hate her but she's my mum. I want to see her.'

'Yes, I understand that,' Gramps said carefully. 'And I don't hate her.'

'That's what you say . . .'

'Because it's the truth,' Gramps replied. 'I'll do it as soon as I get a moment.'

'All right then. Tell me what to do and I'll do it, seeing as how you can't be bothered,' Mike said icily. 'Do I just write to her at the prison?'

'Of course I can be bothered. I said I'd do it and I will.'

'D'you promise?'

'Mike, I hardly think . . .' Nan began.

'I want Gramps to promise,' Mike insisted. He turned back to his grandad. 'Well?'

'I promise. Happy now?'

No. Far from it. But it would have to do – for now. With each passing day, Mike felt like he was hanging on to normality by his fingertips – and his grip was slowly but surely slipping. Everything was so complicated: home, school, his mum, his whole life. How had it all become so complicated? One moment's anger, one single act and his whole world had been turned upside down. It was his mum's fault. She should have got them away from his dad long before things went as far as they did. She'd said as much, admitted to it in court. It wasn't his fault, it was mum's fault. He had to hang on to that. He had to cling on to the fact that he'd done nothing wrong. That was all he had. And if he lost that . . .

35

Gemma
Reparations

'So, Gemma, how was school today?'

'The same as ever.' Gemma shrugged.

Gemma knew without looking up from her homework that her dad was watching her. Since she'd found out about Mum, it seemed like every time she looked up, there he was.

'Why don't you invite a couple of your friends around sometime?' Dad asked.

Gemma's head snapped up.

'I mean, it's just that I never see any of your friends,' Dad carried on.

Gemma ignored the slow burn of embarrassment creeping over her face. 'I didn't think they'd be particularly welcome – especially with you and Tarwin yelling at each other all the time.'

'Of course they'd be welcome. It's your birthday next month. You should have a party.'

Gemma returned to her homework without saying a word.

'Would you like that?'

'What? A party?'

Dad nodded.

'I'll think about it.' Gemma turned so Dad couldn't see her face.

'Would you like some ice-cream after dinner?' asked Dad.

Gemma frowned. 'We don't have any.'

'I could pop to the corner shop and get some,' Dad suggested.

Gemma frowned at him. Well, she'd say one thing for him – he was really trying. Gemma had never had so much attention from her dad. For years she'd wanted him to realise that he had a daughter as well as a son, but now that her wishes were finally coming true, she felt like she was being smothered.

'No, thanks. I'll just have some fruit after dinner,' Gemma stated.

'OK,' said Dad, just a hint of disappointment in his voice.

The front door opened and closed. Footsteps sounded, coming towards the kitchen.

'Hi, Tarwin,' Gemma called out.

Tarwin appeared in the doorway. 'What's all this then?' he grinned.

'We're making dinner.' Dad smiled.

'What is it?'

'Bangers and mash – if that's all right with you, princess?'

Gemma regarded her dad thoughtfully. She'd never heard him call her that before. Try as she might, she couldn't make out what had come over him. And she couldn't figure out why she wasn't pleased at the change in him. She should be jumping for joy but she wasn't. She couldn't work out how she felt. Maybe she didn't feel anything. Maybe that was the problem. Too many months and years of being invisible had left her incapable of feeling anything for anyone – except her mum. And now that was gone too. She wasn't invisible any more – she was a robot. Gemma smiled at the thought. A robot sounded much better. If she was a robot then nothing and no one could hurt her. The ideal position to be in. Yes, that was much better.

'Would you like some dinner?' Dad asked Tarwin.

'Yeah, OK. Go on then.' Tarwin flung his bag down in the corner of the kitchen. 'D'you two need any help?'

Gemma watched Tarwin. He was smiling. Dad was smiling. She was the only one who wasn't. She tried but it felt as if her face was twisting instead of smiling. She tried harder. It felt worse. It wasn't right. It wasn't right that Tarwin and Dad should smile when she couldn't. It wasn't *fair*.

'I wonder what Mum's doing now?' Gemma said to no one in particular.

Immediately the atmosphere in the kitchen changed,

like a light being switched off. Gemma regretted the words as soon as they were out but it was too late to call them back.

'Well, she's not outside the house watching us, that's for sure,' Tarwin said sombrely. The smile had left his face and gone out of his eyes. Now he was giving Dad the look that Gemma recognised of old.

'What d'you mean by that?' Gemma frowned at her brother. What a strange thing to say . . .

'Why don't you ask Dad?' Tarwin replied. 'Don't bother with any dinner for me. I'm not hungry any more.'

As Tarwin left the room, Gemma turned to her dad. 'What's Tarwin talking about? Why would Mum be outside the house watching us?'

Silence. Gemma watched as her Dad's expression slumped.

'It doesn't matter.'

'Tarwin thinks it does,' Gemma pointed out. 'And from the look on your face, so do you.'

No answer.

'Dad?' Gemma prompted.

Her father fumbled for one of the breakfast stools and sat down wearily. Gemma watched in silence, waiting for him to speak. He looked down at the lino for a long time before he at last summoned up the courage to look at her.

'A couple of months after she left, she came back

wanting to see you,' Dad admitted softly. 'Not me. Just you and Tarwin. I . . . I wouldn't even let her in. She started standing outside the house on the opposite side of the road, hoping for a glimpse of you and Tarwin. She'd stand there for hours, not moving.'

Each word her dad spoke was like a push towards the edge of a cliff, and yet Gemma couldn't ask him to stop. She wanted to hear every word. 'I can't remember ever seeing her.'

'I made sure you never did. I thought Tarwin didn't know what was going on, but I caught him waving out of the window to her a couple of times. That's when I'd finally had enough. I told her to stop because she was upsetting you. I told her if she didn't stop, I . . . I'd move somewhere where she'd never find you again. I never saw her after that.'

Gemma felt as if she'd been punched in the stomach. All the air left her body in a painful rush. She stared at her dad, almost unable to take it all in. Her mum was not just alive – she had actually tried to see her and Tarwin. Only Dad had stopped her. How could he? How *dare* he? But Mum shouldn't have given up. If she'd been in her mum's shoes, she wouldn't have let that stop her.

'I don't understand. Why didn't Mum try to get custody of us? She could've done and you wouldn't have been able to stop her.'

Dad looked away, unable to meet her gaze.

'What're you not telling me?' Gemma asked, icily.

'I . . . your mum did try to get custody.' Dad's voice was a quiet monotone. 'But only of . . . Tarwin.'

The final push. And Gemma was falling, falling, falling in total silence. Even her heart was silent. There was no sound. She'd always instinctively known just how devastating the truth could be, but she'd never expected this quiet that came with it. The death of hope. 'I see.'

'No, you don't understand,' Dad said at once. 'After you were born, your mum had a breakdown. Looking back I'm sure it was a severe case of post-natal depression but it meant that she couldn't look after you for a long while. I think she always felt guilty about that and a bit scared of you because of it. I'm sure that's why she felt she could only . . . take care of Tarwin.'

Gemma hardly heard. Dad's words floated past her in a hazy jumble. All she knew, the only fact in her heart and in her head, was that even her own mum hadn't wanted her.

'Gemma? Gemma, you're not listening to me. Your mum loved you too – very much. It was my fault. I was the one who said I'd have her declared mentally unfit to look after a breadstick if she tried to take either of you away from me. She backed down then and in her shoes I would've done exactly the same. For a long while after that, I felt sure she was watching us, but she always made certain that I couldn't see her. So when I couldn't stand it any more, I spent a weekend packing up and we all moved here.'

'That's why Tarwin is always quarrelling with you, isn't it?' Gemma realised. 'He knows what you did . . .'

'I'm not proud of it, Gemma. I did what I thought was best. I was wrong, I know that now, but at the time I was hurting too much to think straight.'

'And you've never seen Mum since?' Gemma asked. Dad shook his head.

'D'you know where she is now?'

Dad shook his head again.

'Is there anything else you and Tarwin know that you're not telling me?' Gemma asked icily.

'No, I . . .'

Gemma turned and walked towards the door.

'Where are you going?'

'To my room.' Gemma carried on walking.

'What about your dinner?' Dad called after her.

'I'm not hungry.'

'Gemma, wait . . .'

Gemma didn't want to hear any more. She didn't care if she never heard another word from Dad again. She ran into her room, slamming the door behind her. She looked down at her hands. They were shaking. Her whole body was shaking. Her head was about to explode. The silence was over.

Do something.

She had to do something to stop herself screaming

till she was hoarse. She went straight over to her bedside table and dug out her mum's scarf from the bottom drawer. Scrunching it in her lap, she stared down at the stars and moon crumpled up all over it. It reminded her of the jumper in *Material Girl*. An idea swirled and found form in Gemma's mind. A horrible idea. She tried to push it away, to dismiss it, but it had taken root and now refused to budge. There was another way to get her jumper, with no danger to herself.

And then, just like that, it wasn't so horrible any more. Well, if the idea wouldn't go away, then she'd use it. And not just use it but embrace it. She'd be like her dad – one of the people in this world who made things happen. Who got what they wanted. Gemma could feel her face set like petrified stone. For the first time she was going to stop fighting against the way things were and not only accept them but use them to her advantage. Wasn't that what everyone else did? She had no one else and she needed no one else. From now on, the only person she was going to care about was herself.

36

Mike
All I Have

Oh, for goodness' sake! He hadn't even set foot in school yet and already she was waiting to hassle him. Mike briefly considered the possibility that Gemma might be standing outside the school gates waiting for someone else, but he dismissed the idea at once. Bowing his head against the driving rain and her, he tried to walk past her. She fell into step with him.

'Mike, d'you know that boutique *Material Girl*, the one around the corner?'

Mike frowned. 'Yes.'

'They've got some lovely jumpers in the window. Dark blue jumpers embroidered with the moon and stars.'

'So?' What was she telling him that for? Like he was the slightest bit interested in jumpers, *Material Girl* or her for that matter.

'I'm a size ten.'

'Fascinating! Excuse me.'

'Could you get me one please?'

'One what?'

'One of the jumpers in *Material Girl*. One of the jumpers with the moon and stars on it.'

Mike glared at her. 'What're you talking about?'

Pause.

'You want me to buy you this jumper?'

Gemma nodded. 'The jumper is fifty pounds.'

Mike froze. Had he heard right? *Fifty pounds?* 'You must be joking.' Mike dug into his pockets and took out his loose change. 'If it costs one pound, seventy-four pence or less you can have it, cos this is all I have in the world. You've seen to that.'

'I want it.'

'Tough. I just told you – I haven't got any money!' Mike shouted. He saw Gemma glance nervously at the people walking past them. The others going into school were curious about their argument, but not curious enough to stop and listen. It was too wet and cold to be nosy. 'You must be living in cloud-cuckoo-land if you think I can get my hands on that kind of money.'

'Then find some other way to get me the jumper.'

'Like how?'

'I'm sure you can think of something.'

And then Mike clicked. No slow, burning realisation. Just a click in his mind and he knew. She wanted him to *steal* it.

'No way,' he said at once.

'I want it, Mike. I want it by tomorrow night or by the weekend everyone will know the truth about you.'

There they were again, those words – *the truth*. Funny how Gemma always used those words to batter at him over and over again.

'I mean it, Mike. I'll tell everyone about you.' Gemma frowned.

'You can't. You wouldn't.'

'Watch me.'

Mike tried to swallow but his throat was now the size of a pinhead.

'Tomorrow afternoon, Mike. I'm giving you a day to come up with the money, but if you can't you'll have to get it some other way,' Gemma told him. 'I'll wait for you outside the shop after school. We'll wait till it opens then you can get it for me. I want that jumper.'

Mike stared at Gemma. How could someone so normal-looking, someone you wouldn't even look at twice for heaven's sake, be so . . . evil? Why was she so determined to make his life a misery? What had he ever done to her?

She walked away. Walked fast. He watched her go, unable to tear his eyes away from her back. How he wished his eyes could send out white-hot lasers or red-hot bullets. A train? A plane? Concorde? A rocket? What would be the fastest way to get away? From Gemma. From Gramps and Nan. From Mum. From everyone. Run away and hide. Mike stood in the pouring rain watching Gemma walk away from him. He wanted to turn and run in the opposite direction.

Run and run and run. And never stop.

37

Gemma
Done It

School was over for another day and she was going home. And . . . well, she had done it. Just as she said she would. She felt nothing – which was good – no, which was *great*. You could get anything you wanted in this world if you didn't feel. It was just a shame that she couldn't feel *happy* about it. She would've settled for feeling satisfaction at what she'd done, but feeling nothing at all was better than feeling bad. If that was all there was, then that was all she wanted or needed.

Gemma turned into her street, her footsteps slowing as she approached her house. She stopped outside her front gate. She didn't want to go in, not just yet. But she had nowhere else to go. She turned and crossed the road to stand opposite her house. Years ago, her mum had stood outside their old home, like this. Just watching.

The cold rain pattered on Gemma's upturned face, the raindrops stinging. A curtain fluttered against the window of her dad's bedroom. At once, Gemma knew that Dad had spotted her and that he was now watching behind the anonymity of white-grey net curtains.

Gemma's expression hardened. What was Dad thinking? He was probably suffering from a severe case of déjà-vu. What would he do now? March outside and tell her to come in with all the force he had once used to tell her mum to stay away? Or maybe he would just stand there and watch from his bedroom window.

With a sigh, Gemma bent her head and crossed the road. Her whole life was suddenly so complicated and instead of trying to make things better, she knew she was making things worse. She felt like she was rolling down a hill – rolling faster and faster, totally out of control. And she knew that when she stopped rolling, the pain would start.

38
Mike
The Letter

When Mike opened the front door, he immediately noticed that something was different. There were no savoury cooking smells wafting towards him from the kitchen, no instant, 'Hi, Mike' or 'We're in here!'

'Nan? Gramps?'

No reply. Then Mike remembered Nan telling him that she and Gramps were going to the local hospital to visit a friend with a broken leg. He was astounded at how disappointed he felt that they weren't here. He was desperate to speak to them. The one time he needed them to be there, they weren't. If Nan and Gramps had been home at that precise moment, he would've told them *everything*. The truth about his mum and dad and all about Gemma. He couldn't steal that jumper. He couldn't steal anything. He'd never stolen anything in his life. Whatever else he might be, he wasn't a thief. But that was exactly what Gemma wanted to make him. Well, he wouldn't do it. He *couldn't*.

You don't have any choice . . .

Mike tried to ignore the words in his head. He did have a choice. Everyone had a choice when you got right down to it. It was a question of what would be his decision. If he told the truth, Gramps and Nan would insist that he tell his story to the police and then it would all come out. It would be in the papers and on the telly and he still wouldn't be able to see Mum. But at least he'd have the satisfaction of stopping Gemma. She'd probably get into a whole load of trouble for trying to . . . to blackmail him. And it was blackmail, wasn't it?

Mike slumped down on the sofa, ignoring the folded note and the money lying on the coffee table before him. What was he going to do? If he told Nan and Gramps and the police, Gemma would probably only get a caution or a reprimand, but his life would be ruined. Every time he thought things couldn't get much worse, they always did. But he wasn't going to let Gemma turn him into a thief.

Slowly, Mike stretched out his arm to pick up the note.

Dear Mikey,

How are you? Did you have a good day at school? You must tell us all about it when we get home. I hope you haven't forgotten that your grandad and I won't be home until around nine tonight.

133

There's some cold ham and chicken in the fridge but in case that doesn't appeal, I've left you some money so you can get some fish and chips or a pizza or a takeaway curry. Please don't buy crisps and sweets and other such nonsense – that isn't proper food and will only rot your teeth. I suggest you eat a good meal first then do your homework. If I were you, I wouldn't put on the television because then you'll feel inclined to watch it.

See you later.
Love, Nan.

Mike forced a smile. Nan wrote the way she spoke. He looked at the money on the table. Two five pound notes. Another forty pounds and he'd be home and dry. Another forty pounds . . . Mike stood up and pulled off his jacket.

Another forty pounds . . .

Would Nan and Gramps have that kind of money lying around the house somewhere? It wouldn't be stealing – not really. He'd take the money but leave them a note promising to replace it. Probably, they'd never even miss it. He'd get a part-time job and pay it back, with interest. Gramps and Nan wouldn't lose out, he'd see to that. They'd get their money back eventually. Besides, from the look of the house and the fridge and cupboards always being full and their big car, Gramps and Nan weren't exactly short of a penny or two. But Mike needed the money now – well, tomorrow afternoon at any rate. If they had it, he'd borrow it, that's all. He'd start from the top of the house and work his way down. All he needed was another forty pounds.

Don't be so stupid, said a voice in his head. Mike ignored it and made his way upstairs.

Ten minutes later he was going through Nan and Gramps's wardrobe. He'd already looked under their mattress and through the drawers of their dressing table. Their fitted wardrobe ran from one side of the room to the opposite wall. Nan had her clothes on one side and Gramps had his on the other. The rail upon which the clothes hung was quite high up – that way there was a lot of room beneath the skirts and shirts and jumpers for shoes and shoeboxes and hangers and other odds and ends. There were shelves at either end of the wardrobe for jumpers and underwear and bedlinen and all the other things Nan didn't want to hang up. Mike wondered where he should start. In Gramps's jacket pockets? Or maybe in Nan's spare handbags. He hesitated over the decision. Maybe he should just wait and ask Gramps and Nan for the money when they came home. But they'd want to know why he wanted so much money and then what? No, that wouldn't work. This way he could buy himself a couple of weeks until he had time to replace the money.

Mike glanced down and a strange thing caught his eye. Beneath the lowest shelf on Nan's side of the wardrobe there was a silver Humpty-Dumpty. There was no other way to describe it. Sure his eyes were playing tricks on him, Mike bent down for a closer look. No, he was right. It *was* a silver-plated Humpty-Dumpty about twenty centimetres high. Mike picked it up and shook it. A smothered rattle sounded. Mike turned it this way and that in his hands. It looked smooth but bits of it were jagged and quite rough against his fingers. He saw the join where Humpty-Dumpty sat on the silver wall beneath. Tugging with all his might, at last the head came off! Rolled-up papers and a gold ring with a single sapphire flew out on to the carpet.

Mike picked up the ring first. It was so beautiful. The stone was of the deepest blue and sparkled like Sirius. Mike put the ring back in Humpty-Dumpty. He gathered up the papers which were now scattered across the floor and had started rolling them up when a word on one of the pieces of paper caught his eye – *Prison*. Ignoring his heart which had started to hammer painfully in his chest, Mike unrolled that particular sheet of paper. He suddenly felt almost unbearably hot. It took a few moments to focus on anything but the words at the top because the letter was written on Amstead Prison headed paper. His mum was in Amstead Prison. Mike began to read.

Dear Robert and Angela,

I've made my decision. I'm sorry but I don't want
to see Mike whilst I'm in here – at least not for
a while. Not for a long while. Tell him I love him
very much and that he's not to blame for any of
what happened, but I don't want him in this place.
It would break his heart – and that would break
mine. When I've got myself together, I'll write and
explain my feelings to him, but I can't yet. Please
tell him that I'm not turning my back on him and
he'll always be the one thing in this world that I
love more than my own life.

But I won't sign a visiting order and that's final.
This is hard enough as it is. Every day I have to
hold on so tight I feel that one sneeze would
shatter every bone in my body. Seeing Mike
would be the last straw, for both of us. Please,
please don't ask me again.

And, Robert and Angela, I hope that one day
you will find it in your hearts to forgive me for
what I did to your son. I don't expect miracles,
not any more. If you decide that you'll never
forgive me, believe me I'll understand, but please
don't blame Mikey in any way for what
happened. Although I never really got the chance
to get to know both of you as well as I would've
liked, I really don't think either of you would do

such a thing, but I believe now it's best to get these things out into the open. That was my mistake with Ricky. When he lost his job and started drinking, I should've put my foot down then but I didn't – with tragic consequences for all of us. So take care of Mikey for me. Give him a chance and you'll find out that he is a lovely, loving boy. Don't tell him that I refused to see him. I'll trust both of you to come up with a reasonable excuse. Give Mikey my love. He'll have it always. But I don't want to see him.

Yours truly, Marsha.

Mike read it and read it and read it again. It was only when he saw drops of water falling on the paper that he realised he was crying. He rolled up the letter slowly and put it away with all the others.

His mum didn't want to see him.

She'd written as much to Nan and Gramps. Gramps had lied. He'd made it seem like he hadn't written to Mike's mum and all the time . . . all the time his mum didn't want to see him. She said she loved him but actions spoke louder than words. She *did* blame him. What other reason could there be for refusing to let him visit her? Mike had always thought that maybe she might blame him. It was the ultimate thing he feared.

But thinking it and seeing it written down in his mum's own handwriting were two different things.

His mum didn't want to see him.

There was no room for any other thought in his mind.

His mum didn't want to see him.

Nothing else mattered but that. He didn't care about anything else. And in that moment, Mike decided that whatever happened to him now, whatever he got, he deserved.

39

Gemma
Nothing

Gemma stood outside *Material Girl*, reading her magazine and occasionally looking up and down the street. The afternoon was bright and very warm to the point of being muggy. Maybe the sunshine was a good omen? Strange, but she didn't feel in the slightest bit anxious. She didn't feel sick either. Late last night, she'd decided that feeling nothing was a wonderful feeling in itself. Even nothing was something. She'd get the jumper . . . correction, *Mike* would get her the jumper and that would be only the beginning. She'd be able to get anything she wanted, anything in the world. And all she had to do was ask Mike.

So where was he? He was late. Gemma turned back to her magazine. She frowned down at the page before her. She'd been reading the same page for the last fifteen minutes and she still had no idea what it said. She had to concentrate. *She* had nothing to be afraid of.

Five minutes passed. Gemma still had no idea what she was reading. With a sigh she closed the magazine.

Someone was standing in front of her. Mike. Gemma gave a start of surprise. She hadn't even heard him arrive. How long had he been standing there? Having him appear just like that was disconcerting, to say the least. She'd wanted to set her expression before he arrived. Now he could see she was flustered and embarrassed.

'I'm here. Now what?' Mike asked, his voice glacial.

'You get me what I want.' Gemma hoped she had matched his tone.

'So you haven't changed your mind?'

'What d'you think?'

'I think you're the nastiest piece of work I've ever met. You should've met my dad. You two would've got on like a house on fire.'

Gemma swallowed hard before she could trust herself to speak. The remark had darted under her defences, hurting her – but she was OK now. But the fact that he'd been able to get to her at all was alarming. What had happened to not feeling anything? Another illusion? Or was the word – delusion?

'Well, what happens now?'

Gemma shrugged and pointed to the shop door. 'In you go.'

'You're still determined to force me to do this?'

'I'm not forcing you. You have a choice. You don't have to do it,' Gemma told him.

'And if I don't, you'll ruin my life – and the lives of all my family,' Mike said bitterly. 'That's some choice.'

Gemma shrugged again. 'You'd better go in and get the jumper before the shop closes. Remember, I'm a size ten.'

'I don't give a stuff what size you are.'

'You will if you come out of the shop with a jumper that's the wrong size,' Gemma told him.

After giving her the filthiest, bitterest look she'd ever seen in her life, Mike entered the shop. A chime sounded as the door opened, then closed. The moment he was out of sight, Gemma felt strange. A feeling crept over her, so slowly at first that she had trouble working out what it was. Beads of perspiration broke out all over her body like tiny pinpricks, making her skin itch. Her palms were moist and her stomach was churning like a food processor. Her mouth filled up with saliva. Gemma swallowed. It filled again.

She watched the closed shop door, wondering what was going on. She took a step closer, then another. She was at the shop window now but she couldn't see a thing. Cupping her hands around her face, Gemma tried to get a closer look. The churning in her stomach was getting worse. Why couldn't she see Mike? Where was he? What was he doing?

40

Mike
Moon And Stars

'Can I help you?'

The shop assistant was at his side the moment he entered the shop.

'I ... er ... I was looking for a present for my ... my mu ... sister,' Mike stammered.

The shop assistant smiled at him. 'What did you have in mind?'

'A ... a jumper. She wants a jumper.'

'We have some lovely ones over here ...'

'No, er ... she wanted a specific one. It's navy blue and it's got the moon and stars on it.'

'The only ones we've got like that are these ones for fifty pounds,' the shop assistant said doubtfully. 'That's a lot of money. Maybe your mum and dad will chip in. You could give your sister the present from all of you.'

'You can put a deposit down now if you like.' A voice sounded behind Mike, making him jump. He turned quickly, to see the friendly, smiling face of a reed-thin, reed-tall beautiful black woman with her hair pulled

143

back into a pony tail and tied with a long, flowing scarf. This woman looked like she didn't have on a thing that cost under fifty pounds. She was immaculate. She reminded Mike of someone but for the life of him, he couldn't figure out who.

'The deposit will ensure we keep the jumper for you whilst you have a word with your parents and, if you decide not to buy it, we'd give you back your money. But it's entirely up to you.'

Mike looked at the jumpers hanging on the circular rack. They were just navy blue jumpers with bits of silver and gold ribbon sewn onto them. Nice enough but certainly not fifty pounds worth of nice. At least, not as far as he could tell. Why was Gemma so determined to get one of them? Or maybe the jumper wasn't the most important thing? Maybe Gemma just wanted him to jump through hoops for her and this was one way to do it.

'Do you have a size ten?'

The shop assistant had a look. 'You're lucky. This is the last one left.'

She held it up for him to have a closer look. Somewhere in the distance, a telephone rang.

Mike took the hanger from the shop assistant as she turned away to answer the phone. He held up the jumper and looked at it. If he had any sense he would hand it back, thank the women and get out of there as fast as he could. But Gemma was outside, with her threat hanging over him like the sword of Damocles.

'Mrs Spiner, phone call for you,' a voice called from beyond the fitting room.

The immaculately dressed woman turned and headed in the direction of the phone and the voice. Mike looked up at the shop assistant.

'I'll leave you to have a look around and make up your mind.' The shop assistant smiled.

'Thank you,' Mike said gratefully.

How was he going to do this? He had no idea. The jumper was on a hanger, so his first job was to get it off. Since it was round-necked, there was no way he could do it easily. He might've got away with it if he was a girl cos then he'd have had the excuse of trying it on. Mike put it back on the rack. The shop assistant caught his eye and smiled at him again, then she turned back to opening a large brown cardboard box. Mike looked around. No one was watching. He picked up the jumper again and pulled it off the hanger. Rolling it into a ball, he stuffed it under his jacket beneath his left arm and headed straight for the door.

41

Gemma
Worth It

Gemma's focus adjusted. She was no longer looking
through the window, but staring at her reflection in the
glass. Her normal, everyday face had vanished, to be
replaced by a mask of total misery. She swallowed past
the pain in her chest and carried on looking at herself.
All this was supposed to make her happy, to get her
what she wanted come hell or high water. But look at
her. It was as if her sanity, her very life was blowing up
in her face. And it occurred to her in that moment that
she wasn't what her mum had made her, or even what
her dad had made her. Everything she was now, she'd
done to herself. There was no blinding flash of light, no
thunderbolts from the sky, just the certain knowledge
that for once she was telling herself the truth. She had
turned herself into something she wasn't, to stop herself
from being hurt. And all she'd done was hurt herself
worse. It was as if she'd literally cut off her nose to
spite her face.

She had to do something. Now. At once. Something

to make things right, to put things – and herself – back to normal. Otherwise she'd be lost for ever, stuck in a twisting spiral of unhappiness and guilt.

Taking a deep breath, Gemma took a step towards the door, then froze as it opened. Mike came out. There was something bulky inside his jacket under one arm. Gemma moved away from him. She backed away, step after step, before turning. But she didn't get the chance to run. The shop door opened again. The chime sounded like a church bell.

'You! Come back here!'

Gemma turned her head. A shop assistant Gemma had never seen before stepped out of the shop and placed a hand on Mike's shoulder. Gemma bent to tie her shoelaces.

'What've you got under your jacket?' the shop assistant asked angrily.

'Nothing. Let me go!' Mike struggled to get away but the shop assistant had him in a vice-like grip.

And then the jumper fell to the ground.

Gemma straightened up. She turned and started walking away.

'Mrs Spiner, call the police!' the shop assistant called back into the shop.

Gemma carried on walking. She wanted to sprint away but she forced herself to walk slowly, calmly.

'You there!' the shop assistant called after her.

Fixing a look of curiosity and nothing else on her face, Gemma turned.

'D'you know this boy?' the shop assistant asked.

Gemma stared at Mike. He looked back at her, not saying a word.

'You're both wearing the same uniform so you must go to the same school,' the shop assistant said with impatience. 'So do you know this . . . this thief?'

Gemma saw Mike flinch at that, as if the shop assistant had hit him.

'Well?'

'No,' Gemma whispered.

'Pardon?'

'No, I don't know him,' Gemma replied.

And then she turned and ran.

42

Mike
Understand

The bench was hard. The room was stifling hot. Mike longed to ask someone to turn the heating down. Why did they keep it so hot? If they didn't turn it down soon, he was going to be sick.

'Are you ready to tell me your name now?'

Mike looked up. A police officer sat behind a large desk. Sergeant Wilson? The sergeant had told Mike his name but Mike had hardly heard him. Wilson . . . Yes, that sounded right.

'M . . . Mi . . .' Mike swallowed hard, then tried again. 'Michael Woods.'

'Good. Now we're getting somewhere.' Sergeant Wilson picked up his pen and started writing. 'And your address?'

Horrified, Mike shook his head. No way. He didn't want Gramps and Nan dragged into this. It had nothing to do with them. And what would happen when they found out? They'd be sorry they took him in. He could just see them now, the look on their faces that would say, 'like mother, like son'. And the worse thing about it was that they would be wrong. He wasn't like his mum. Like his dad maybe, but not his mum. Mum deserved better than the son she'd been lumbered with. If Mike could have snapped his fingers and just ceased to exist then he would have done it at once, with no hesitation.

'Come on, son. What's your address? We'll find out sooner or later so you might as well tell us now.'

Mike bent his head and forced the words out. He couldn't get his voice above a whisper but it didn't matter – the sergeant heard him anyway.

'You live with your mum and dad?'

Mike shook his head. 'My . . . my grandparents.'

'And their names are?'

Mike told him.

'Let's have their digits then.'

Sergeant Wilson waited patiently. Mike reluctantly told him their landline and mobile phone numbers.

'Fine. We'll phone them on one of those numbers now. They can come and pick you up.'

Mike lowered his head. He didn't want to look at anyone. He didn't want to be seen by anyone. Where was he? In something called a custody suite. But how had he got here? He tried to remember but his head was whirling with different images. He couldn't remember everything that had happened, just flashes. Like his mind was taking photographs for a scrapbook rather than recording everything. He remembered the shop assistant pulling him back into the shop. He remembered her fingers biting into his shoulder until his upper arm began to tingle. And he'd never forget the look she'd given him, her whole body rigid with contempt – like he'd just crawled out from underneath a dirty rock.

The police had arrived almost immediately. They cautioned him and it was like something off the telly – except he couldn't hear what they were saying above the sound of his own blood thundering in his ears. One police officer asked him something. Mike could tell that by the expectant look on the officer's face when he finished speaking. Mike hesitated then nodded, but he had no idea what he was agreeing to. The police officer seemed satisfied though. And then Mike was sitting in the back of a police car with two policemen at the front. One kept glancing back and shaking his head.

Mike hadn't spoken at all in the car. His voice had deserted him as sheer panic had washed over him. Now here he was at the police station, in a room with a bench against the wall and another police officer behind a desk. He'd been asked a lot of questions, most of them at least three times before they'd sunk in. It had taken a long while before he found his voice again.

Mike leaned his head back against the wall, his eyes closed. He missed his mum so much it hurt. If only he could do something, *anything*, to stop it from hurting . . .

Someone was sitting down next to him. Mike opened his eyes. It was Gramps and Nan. Gramps was shaking his head. Nan opened her arms and without hesitation Mike moved into them. She hugged him so tightly that he could hardly breathe, but he didn't care. He didn't want to move.

'I'm trying to understand, Mike. Help me to understand. Tell me why you did it,' said Gramps.

Mike wanted to cover his ears and close his eyes. He desperately wanted to get away from the hurt in Gramps's voice. He drew away from Nan to see her quickly look away so that she could wipe her eyes. That was even worse.

'I don't understand,' Gramps said again. 'Why would you want to . . . to take a jumper – and a woman's jumper at that?'

Mike didn't answer. He studied well-worn dark blue carpet beneath his feet.

'Mike, why did you do it?' Nan asked again. 'Tell us why.'

Because I had no choice. Because I didn't want you to think even worse of me. Because I didn't want you to find out the real truth about me – the truth that I hide from everyone, but which Gemma has discovered.

Which reason should he give? One of them? All of them? Mike kept silent.

'I am so ashamed.' Gramps couldn't keep the bitterness out of his voice. 'I have never, *ever* even set foot inside a police station. And now I'm here because my grandson takes it into his head to become a thief.'

Silence.

'Have you ever stolen anything from a shop before?'

Mike looked at him.

'Well? Have you?'

'No. Never,' he whispered.

'Then why in heaven's name did you decide to start now? If you needed a jumper why didn't you say? Your nan and I would've bought you one.'

'I'm sorry.'

'Sorry!' Gramps spluttered over the word. 'Sorry and a pound might get me half a cup of coffee – but not much else.'

Mike looked away. Gramps was right. Sorry was a useless word. Inadequate and pathetic. Mike had spent the last year saying sorry. Sorry to Mum. Sorry to Mum. Sorry to Mum. And she was still in prison. Sorry didn't change anything.

43

Gemma
Make It Right

Gemma stood outside Mike's front door, trying to find the courage to ring the doorbell. She'd been standing there for the last half-hour and she still hadn't summoned up the nerve to do it.

Come on. Get on with it, she told herself sternly.

It was dark now and cold. Gemma looked up at the clear, dark sky. There seemed to be only one star out there. No, tell a lie . . . The longer she looked, the more stars she could see. Until the sky was almost more silver than evening blue. Millions of stars, shining for millions of years.

Taking a deep breath, Gemma pressed on the doorbell before she could change her mind. A light appeared in the hall. Gemma swallowed hard. It would be so easy to turn around and run all the way home, but she couldn't.

The door opened. A wave of warmth rushed out to meet her. An elderly woman stood at the door. She wore a blue skirt and a frilly white blouse and she had a face which looked like it smiled easily. But not at the moment. She frowned when she saw Gemma.

'Hello. Is . . . is Mike in?'

'He's getting ready to go to bed.' The woman looked at Gemma curiously.

'You must be Mike's grandmother. I'm Gemma. I'm Mike's . . . I'm in Mike's class.' Gemma took another deep breath. 'Can I see him please?'

'I don't think so.' Mike's grandmother shook her head. 'You can see him tomorrow in school.'

'Oh, please. It's really important.'

'No. We've all had a . . .'

'It won't take long, I promise. *Please?*'

Mike's nan studied her. Long moments passed. 'Come in then,' she said at last.

Gemma stepped slowly into the house. The front door shutting behind her made her jump.

'Mike? Mike, there's someone here to see you,' Mike's nan called up the stairs.

Moments later Mike's head appeared over the upstairs banister. His expression clouded over the moment he laid eyes on Gemma. 'What are you doing here? What d'you want?'

'Mike!' his nan admonished.

'Can I talk to you . . . please?' Gemma asked. She didn't even try to keep the desperation out of her voice. He had to talk to her, he just had to.

'No. I've got nothing to say to you. And if you've

come to gloat you can at least do it from outside my own house.'

'I didn't come to gloat.'

'D'you know something about that business earlier?' Mike's nan asked. Her eyes narrowed as she regarded Gemma. 'Who did you say you were again?'

'Gemma. Gemma Elliott.' Gemma could feel her face getting redder.

'Are you Mike's girlfriend then?' said Mike's nan.

Gemma had never been so embarrassed. '*No!* No. No,' she replied quickly. 'I . . . no.'

'Do you know what happened earlier?' the elderly woman asked again.

Mike came charging downstairs, oblivious to the fact that he was in his pyjamas. 'Nan, it's OK. I'll talk to her. You can go back into the sitting room now.'

'I . . .' Whatever else his nan was, she wasn't stupid. It was obvious that Mike wanted to talk to Gemma alone.

Gemma forced herself to stand her ground. Mike looked like he wanted to pick her up bodily and toss her out the door.

'Would you like a drink whilst you're here?' Mike's nan asked.

'No, thank you.' Gemma shook her head. Her gaze returned to Mike who waited until his grandmother had gone back into the sitting room before he spoke.

'Happy now? Have you got what you wanted?' Mike whispered bitterly.

'What d'you mean?'

'I was taken to the police station.'

'I . . . I never meant . . .'

'I don't want to hear it. I want you to leave. Just go. And don't come back.'

'Mike, please. I came here to say . . . to say I'm sorry. I . . . I wasn't thinking straight.'

'Oh yes you were!' Mike shot back. 'You wanted the jumper or you wanted me to get into trouble, you didn't particularly mind which.'

Gemma opened her mouth to argue but the words wouldn't come – because he was right, and they both knew it.

'Well, for your information the police cautioned me. I'm sure you're sorry I didn't get arrested and taken into custody immediately. That would have suited you, wouldn't it?'

'No, I . . . I'm glad they didn't arrest you,' Gemma told him.

But Mike hardly heard her. 'Of course Gramps and Nan are bitterly disappointed in me. They'll probably never trust me out of their sight again. Gramps has spent the last two hours telling me how he's never been so ashamed, and Nan . . . and Nan . . .' Mike's voice choked up. Gemma saw him swallow hard. 'Nan was *crying*.'

'Mike, I . . .' Gemma's hand was touching Mike's arm before she knew what was happening.

Mike sprung back as if her hand had suddenly turned white-hot. 'Get out. Go on. Get lost!'

Gemma's hand dropped to her side. She wanted to say so many things but no words would come.

She didn't get the chance to say anything else. Mike turned around and went back upstairs. Gemma watched him until he was out of sight, then she let herself out of the house. It was going to be a long walk home.

44

Mike
Everyone Knows

Mike opened the door. Immediately, the whole class-room went quiet. Every eye was upon him.

Everyone knows, Mike realised, anguished.

What should he do? Bending his head so that all he could see was the floor, Mike walked to his desk. He sat down. Kane moved his bag away from Mike to the other side of the table.

Silence.

'Is it true you were caught stealing from *Material Girl*?' Kane asked. His voice rang out in the stillness like the peal of a bell.

Mike looked at Kane. He looked around the room. They were all waiting for his answer.

'I didn't,' Mike denied.

How had they all found out? Gemma. She must've carried out her threat to tell everyone. On top of every-thing else, she'd told on him. Mike turned around to glare at her. Gemma shook her head slowly. Confused, Mike turned to face the rest of the class.

'What did the police do when they took you to the police station?' Kane continued.

'I'm not a thief,' Mike repeated.

'Yes you are. My mum owns *Material Girl*,' Robyn called from across the room. 'She told me all about it. I couldn't believe it when she told me the name of the boy the police had taken away.'

'I . . .' Shocked, now at last Mike realised why the owner of *Material Girl* looked so familiar. And why Gemma had insisted he took the jumper from *that* shop in particular. It was Gemma's way of getting back at Robyn for not receiving an invite to Robyn's birthday party. And she'd used him to do her dirty work. She really did hate him – and everyone else in the class.

'Mum said you're not to come anywhere near me or her shop again,' Robyn added coldly. 'She's going to come up the school and ask if I can be put into another class.'

'I'm not a thief!' Mike hissed. 'Leave me alone.'

'Gladly.' Robyn turned away, but not before she made sure that her expression told Mike exactly what she thought of him.

Mike shouted at the others who were still watching him. '*I'm not a thief.*'

They didn't believe him. But he wasn't. *He wasn't*. If it hadn't been for Gemma, he would never have taken the jumper. The thought would never have entered his head. Inside, in his heart, he wasn't a thief. In his heart he was . . . something much worse.

Mr Butterworth breezed into the room. 'Sorry I'm late, everyone. OK, English books open. We're going to study chapter twelve today.'

Mike dug into his bag to get out his workbook. When he looked up, Kane was watching him.

'I never figured you for a thief,' Kane said in a matter-of-fact voice.

'Don't tell me. Let me guess. You don't want to be friends any more.'

'We can still be friends.' Kane shrugged.

But not the same kind of friends as we were before, Mike realised.

What was he going to do now? Up in Darlington, once his mum had been arrested he'd been treated like a leper until the only choice left open to him was to get harder than those around him. It'd been his only way to survive. He'd thought that moving down here to live with Gramps and Nan would make things different. He wouldn't have to pretend to be someone he wasn't any more. He could be himself. But that hadn't worked either.

A spiral of faces swam around him. Gramps's embarrassment. Nan's disappointment. Robyn's scorn. Kane's distrust. How was he supposed to live like this? And he couldn't move on and start again – he had nowhere else to go.

45
Gemma
All Right

Gemma stood a few metres behind Mike, watching as he sat alone on her favourite bench in the school grounds. She walked over to him.

'Mike, are you all right?' she asked.

Gemma waited. Nothing. Moving around the bench to stand directly in front of him, she repeated the question. Still nothing. Gemma wasn't even sure if Mike was aware that she was standing there. And the expression on his face scared her. Because his face was like a mask. It held defeat and nothing else. She recognised that look from seeing it in her own reflection countless times.

'Mike?'

Mike stood up and walked away from her. After a moment's hesitation, Gemma ran to catch up with him. They walked in silence until Gemma realised that Mike was heading for the school gates. It was only lunchtime and he was leaving the school. He would get into awful trouble. He might even get suspended. Gemma would've laughed at her thoughts if they'd been funny. Mike couldn't be in any more trouble. She'd seen to that.

'Mike, where are you going?'

Mike turned to look at her. No, that wasn't true. He turned in her direction but his eyes looked straight through her.

'Nowhere. I'm just going for a walk. Go away.'

'You can't leave school now. Mike, listen.'

'*I said, go away!*' Without warning, Mike shouted at Gemma, making her jump. She took a step back but then held her ground. He wasn't going to get rid of her that easily. But Mike looked straight ahead, ignoring her again. He opened the school gates and stepped out into the street. Gemma looked around desperately but there was no one in sight. No one that she knew. No one she could call on to help her. She had no choice but to follow. She tried to pull Mike back but he shrugged out of her grasp without even looking at her.

'Stop following me,' Mike told her once they'd reached the bottom of the road.

Gemma didn't reply, but no way was she going to let Mike out of her sight. The look on his face frightened her. All the more so because she knew she'd put it there.

They walked for several minutes in silence. Mike strode along as if he was in training for the Olympics. Gemma was beginning to get a stitch but no way was she going to stop now. She concentrated on breathing regularly to get rid of her stitch and keeping up with

Mike. Those were the only two things she had on her mind.

'I said, stop following me!' Mike stopped to glare at her with loathing.

Gemma shook her head.

Mike turned and carried on walking. Did he know where he was going? Gemma didn't think so. She didn't think he even cared. He was just trying to get away. And if she hadn't been with him, he would still be trying to get away. Gemma wondered what she should do. If only he would stop long enough for her to marshal her thoughts.

It was when Mike turned down the canal road that Gemma felt the first grip of fiery panic. Why was he going this way? There was nothing around here but old bits of junk, discarded shopping trolleys and other unsavoury items that no one wanted to take a closer look at, tipped into the canal. The canal ran frothily shallow and nasty in some places – murky, deep and dark in others. A footbridge at least a storey high over the deep water was the only bridge for about three-quarters of a kilometre. And even the footbridge was disgusting. Filthy and covered in graffiti, it was an eyesore to say the least. Gemma hadn't been to this part of the canal in close to a year and it hadn't changed. If anything it had got worse. So why was Mike here? His grandparents didn't live in this part of town.

Mike walked on to the bridge over the canal but

stopped halfway across. Gemma stood at his side, watching as Mike looked down into the murky brown-grey water metres below them. Panic had now been overtaken by choking fear. Why had he stopped? She hadn't wanted him to walk on to the footbridge but now that they were here, Gemma longed for him to keep on moving.

They stood in silence for what seemed like for ever. Gemma because she could think of nothing to say, and Mike because as far as he was concerned, Gemma wasn't even there. He was alone in his utter misery. He was nowhere. Gemma could read every line and curve on Mike's face. It was like looking into the window of *Material Girl* all over again.

'It's meant to be quite deep here,' Mike said softly. He wasn't talking to her, he was talking to himself.

He wasn't going to do anything stupid, was he? *Please don't let him do anything stupid.*

'It might not be that deep. It's too dirty for anyone to really tell.' Gemma's words fell out in a breathless rush.

'So it's drown or break your neck . . .' Mike had a strange, faraway smile on his face. A smile that froze Gemma's blood in her veins.

Please don't let him do anything stupid . . .

Could she stop him if he decided to do something . . . rash? Gemma didn't think so. And worse than feeling so ineffectual, was the knowledge that he was here because of *her*. If anything did happen to him, how would she ever live with that fact? She couldn't. She wouldn't be able to.

'Mike, let's go back to school – OK?'

'I'm never going back there.' There was a finality about his words that chilled Gemma to the bone.

'Mike, listen. I'm sorry. Let me tell everyone the truth. It wasn't your fault. Once I tell everyone that, I'm sure they'll understand.'

'Just like you understood?'

Gemma wasn't sure what to say. 'Mike, let's go back to school. We'll go to Mr Butterworth and I'll tell him the truth – I promise.'

'I haven't got any more money.'

'I don't want your money!' Gemma shouted at him. 'Shut up about money.'

'Then what do you want from me? I haven't got anything else.'

'I . . .'

'It doesn't matter. Go away, Gemma. I need to be alone.'

Gemma's heart stopped beating. 'What d'you mean?'

'Just what I said. You'll have to find someone else to torment.' Mike laughed bitterly. 'That's my one consolation at least. You won't be able to touch me.' Mike pulled his bag off his shoulder and dumped it on the bridge.

Gemma grabbed his arm. 'Mike, please. Let's just go back to school.'

'So you can tell Mr Butterworth the truth?'

'Yes. I will, I promise.'

Mike's eyes burned into her. 'Well, you'll have to have your fun without me. Go and tell him the truth on your own.'

Mike pushed himself up with his hands to sit down on the waist-high wall that formed the barrier on either side of the bridge. He sat with his back to the canal, his legs dangling down over his school bag.

'I just need to be alone,' he whispered to himself.

Gemma glanced down into the canal water, but she couldn't bear to look at it and turned away. Could Mike swim? The answer came to her as plain as day.

Not if he didn't want to.

Gemma could only swim about three strokes before she was in trouble. And there was still no one around. Mike closed his eyes, his head tilted back. Gemma watched as he took one deep breath, then another and another. His fingers stretched and relaxed as he moved his fingertips over the rough wall. Then his hands were still. Somewhere in the distance came the rough cry of a crow. Mike turned his head towards it. But only for a moment. He swallowed hard, then swallowed again. It was as if he was allowing each of his senses to focus just one last time. He leaned forward slightly, then leaned back. His body seemed suddenly boneless, swaying in the slight breeze as if it had no will of its own.

All he had to do was lean backwards a little bit more . . . All he had to do was push back with his hands . . . Gemma tried to force the image out of her head. She told herself she was being stupid, she had too much imagination. Mike wasn't going to do anything like the horrific pictures she had in her head. But her hand reached out for him and her stomach lurched sickeningly. She didn't touch him, she didn't dare. That might send him over the edge just as much as one wrong word.

'Mike, what're you going to do?' Gemma looked around but there was no one near. There was nothing. Just a warm summer's day and a feeling of desperation and a deep, murky canal. She watched nervously as Mike stopped swaying. He looked straight at her.

'Why are you still here?'

Gemma couldn't answer.

'Turn around and run away – you're good at that. You don't even have to tell anyone that you saw me.'

And still Gemma couldn't speak.

'Go on. Go back to school. Tell Mr Butterworth the truth about me.' Mike's voice was a monotone. 'Tell him it wasn't Mum who killed my dad. It was me. Go and tell him.'

46

Mike
Jealous

'What . . . what're you talking about?' Gemma's hand fell to her side. She stared at Mike, profoundly shocked.

Puzzled, Mike frowned at her. Why did she have that look on her face? Like she didn't know. His frown turned into a scowl of disbelief. 'Don't play games, Gemma. Go back and tell Mr Butterworth the truth. I'm not going to be around to care.'

'*You killed your dad?*' Gemma's expression hadn't changed. Her eyes were still as wide as saucers and her mouth was hanging open.

'Oh, come on. You knew that already,' Mike dismissed.

'I didn't. I didn't know anything of the kind,' Gemma denied vigorously.

'What're you going on about? You've been threatening to tell everyone the truth about me since I had the bad luck to end up in your class.'

'But I was talking about . . . the way you didn't want anyone to know about your mother, about her being in prison. It was obvious you were ashamed of her. That's what I was talking about.'

Mike regarded Gemma with suspicion but the look on her face couldn't have been feigned.

'So you really didn't . . .' Mike's voice trailed away.

'Of course not. I don't know your mum or any of your family. I didn't know you until you came to our school. How could I have known about . . . about the rest?'

Silence.

'Did you really . . .?' Gemma lowered her voice. 'Did you really kill your dad?'

Mike swallowed hard. He looked at Gemma and nodded.

'What happened? I won't tell anyone, I promise.'

'Yeah, right!' Mike sniffed with derision.

'I won't. I know you have no reason to believe me or trust me, but I won't tell a soul.'

'Why not? You could blackmail me until I'm ninety with that bit of information,' Mike said bitterly.

'I wouldn't do that.'

'Oh no?' Mike's expression told all too clearly what he thought of that statement.

'Don't look at me like that,' Gemma said bitterly. 'I think I must've gone crazy for a while, but I'm not crazy now – I promise you. You don't know what it's been like. I have no friends and school is just as bad as home. It's hell having people look through you and past you like you're not even there. Like you're invisible.'

'It's worse to have them look at you all the time, like you're under a microscope,' Mike told her.

'You don't know how lucky you are,' Gemma said. 'You've got a family – your mum and your grandparents all care about you. You matter. You make a difference to other people's lives. I never have. At least you know you're real. At least you know you *exist*. But I couldn't say the same thing about me. I was really beginning to wonder. When someone dies they say that they're still alive as long as they're remembered. Well, I'm alive and no one noticed me or cared I was around – even my dad and my brother. They didn't bother – until I found out that Dad had chased Mum away. She wasn't dead at all. Then he noticed me but only because he had a guilty conscience and that was worse. You don't know what it's like to be invisible. It's like being dead and forgotten. It's like never living at all. You try living like that for a while.'

Mike glared at her, unable to hide what he was feeling. 'I've never heard such a load of twaddle. You're so full of self-pity there's no room for anything else, is there?'

'You don't understand . . .'

'I understand perfectly. Because you were hurting, you wanted everyone else to hurt too. Your mum left you. And everything bad that's happened to you and everything bad you've ever done is because of that. It's your mum's fault. It's your dad's fault. It's the man-in-the-moon's fault.'

'I never said that,' Gemma denied, tears pricking behind her eyes. 'If I want someone to blame, I'll look in a mirror. I've figured that much out for myself.'

'Then why go after me?' asked Mike, looking out across the canal water. 'What did I do to you?'

'I knew something about you and you couldn't ignore me.' Gemma lowered her head. Her words were a whisper now. 'It's difficult to explain, but I was a real, live person to you. And I wanted someone to pay for all those people who thought I was . . . was nothing.'

'So it was just my luck to be in the wrong place at the wrong time?' Mike said with contempt.

'No. It wasn't *you*. It could've been anyone.'

'So it wasn't me personally?'

'Oh no. I like you. I mean . . .' Gemma broke off in confused embarrassment.

'You *like* me? If all this is you liking me, I'd hate to see what you'd do if you hated my guts.' Mike frowned.

Gemma smiled, a smile that faded almost immediately. Mike stared at her. What was so amusing? Then he realised what he'd said. And whilst he didn't smile, the despair that'd been crippling him for so long was now somehow, if not bearable, then certainly less. He had no idea why. Gemma knew about him and he'd been the one to tell her. He should feel worse, but somehow he didn't. Maybe because he'd reached as low as he could go. What else could she do to him?

'Mike, I never hated you,' Gemma said quietly. 'I think that was part of the problem.'

'I'm not with you.'

'You're all the things I'm not. You make friends easily. You're not shy. People automatically like you.'

Mike watched as Gemma lapsed into silence. She was looking at him but Mike knew that at that moment she wasn't *seeing* him. Her gaze was turned inward.

'I think that in a way I was jealous,' Gemma said quietly. 'I didn't mean to . . . It all just got out of hand. And it was easier for me to pretend I didn't care.'

Mike understood that perfectly. He'd told himself the same thing when he went into *Material Girl*.

'So what happened to your dad?' Gemma asked.

Mike considered. It was a strange thing, but now he did want to tell her.

'Did you really kill him?'

One word. 'Yes.'

47

Gemma
Protection

Gemma waited for Mike to continue. She sensed that if she asked any more he would withdraw from her. It had been so hard to tell him all those things about herself, things she had never told anyone else. Some of them she hadn't even admitted to herself. But it was right that she tell Mike. It was peculiar but Gemma could think of no one else she *could* tell.

'Dad was made redundant about five years ago,' Mike said at last. 'That's not an excuse. That's just part of the reason.'

Gemma nodded.

'He tried to set up on his own and lost his redundancy money. He tried to get the money back but he just lost more.'

'How did he try to get it back?'

'By betting on anything that moved,' Mike said with contempt. 'For a while I'd spend every evening listening to Mum and Dad argue about money, money, money. At first, they'd go into their bedroom to quarrel and I'd have to listen at the door. But after a while they stopped caring whether I heard or not.'

Gemma found herself wondering about why her own mum had gone away. Had it been as bad between her and Dad?

'Then Dad starting playing his games. We couldn't eat dinner without him and he'd turn up later and later each evening and then complain the food was inedible. If Mum and I were ever watching anything on the telly, he'd switch it over. He had to show us who was the boss. And he started hitting Mum. The first time he swore there'd never be a repeat. He cried and cried. But after that he started drinking. That was his excuse to do it again.' Mike snorted derisively. 'It sounds like a soap or something, doesn't it? But it wasn't. It was my life – and my mum's and dad's. He gave Mum and me lists of things to do. They had to be done in order and on time or there'd be hell to pay. It took months and months but Mum finally had enough. She packed up our stuff and we were going to leave.'

'How did you feel about that?'

'Glad,' Mike said fiercely. 'I never wanted to see him again. Not after what he'd put Mum and me through.'

'What happened?'

'Mum was in the car and we were all ready to go, but then I insisted on going back into the house because we'd forgotten Brewster.'

'Brewster?'

'Our cat. I went back into the house, into the sitting room to get him, and Dad was there. He'd come in the back way. He took one look at me and he instantly knew what was going on. He asked where Mum was and I told him she was outside in the car. I'll never forget his face . . .' Mike looked away over the canal.

Gemma opened her mouth to speak, only to close it without saying a word.

'He was frightened, actually frightened. You see, Mum had threatened to leave plenty of times before, but she'd never done anything about it. Dad tried to push past me. I knew what he was going to do. He was going to try and persuade Mum to stay . . . I didn't want Mum and me to live with him. I was desperate. I pulled him back and he shrugged me off. So I . . . so I pushed him.'

'What d'you mean?' Gemma frowned.

'I pushed him – hard. To this day I'm not sure why. I think I wanted him to turn around and lash out at me. I wanted to have some bruises to show Mum so she wouldn't give in. Only he . . . he fell against the window-sill and hit his head. When he didn't move, I . . . I . . . panicked. I ran back to the car and we left.'

'You didn't tell your mum what had happened?'

Mike shook his head.

'Why not?' Gemma asked.

'I don't know.' Mike shrugged, not looking at her. 'No, that's not true. I do know. I wanted to get away from Dad and that house and the whole street just as fast and as far as I could. I didn't think he was that badly hurt. I reckoned he'd just knocked himself out for a while and by the time he woke up, Mum and I would be long gone.'

Silence.

'When did your mum find out?'

'When it was on the news.' Mike sighed. 'Mrs Everett, our neighbour, saw Dad go in the back door and heard Mum drive away soon afterwards. When she found Dad she put two and two together.'

'And made thirty-seven,' said Gemma. 'What happened to your dad was an accident.'

'But it wasn't. Don't you see? I'd wished he'd disappear or die for so long and then it happened, because of me.'

'You pushed him and he fell. It was an accident,' Gemma insisted. 'It didn't happen because you wished it – unless you had a genie or a leprechaun in your pocket at the time.'

Mike looked at her then, her comment bringing him out of the past and back into the present. 'When I told Mum what'd really happened she said that the police would never believe me. She said that if and when they caught up with us, I was not to say anything. I was to let her do all the talking.'

'And she took the blame?'

Mike nodded. 'By the time I realised what she was

doing, I tried to tell the police the truth but they thought I was just trying to cover up for Mum. And then she made me promise that I wouldn't tell anyone what had really happened. She said it would ruin my life.' Mike gave a brittle laugh. 'What a joke!'

'And then you met me and I made things worse,' Gemma said sombrely. She shook her head.

'That doesn't matter now.'

The minutes ticked by as neither of them spoke.

Gemma looked down into the canal. 'You're not going to . . . to do anything stupid, are you?'

Mike jumped down off the bridge wall and followed Gemma's gaze to look down at the canal. Just one word. 'No.'

An icy shiver raced through Gemma's body. If she hadn't been there . . . 'If you had . . . done it, you'd have been taking me with you.'

Mike turned to her. He didn't need to ask her what she meant. 'Maybe that was the whole point. I would've done it, you know.'

'I know.'

They both stood looking out over the wall into the water below.

'So you've never told anyone about your dad?' Gemma asked.

'No, not since the police and the probation officers didn't believe me. And when Mum found out what I was saying she told me to stop at once. She ordered me never to repeat my "story" to anyone else,' Mike replied.

'I've never had anyone to talk to about how I was feeling either,' Gemma admitted.

And it was then that Gemma realised the pain in her chest had gone. She looked at Mike. He didn't look much like a safety valve but that's what he was. Maybe that was what she was too. They'd both had so much inside them with no way to release it, that sooner or later it had to explode out. Gemma wondered what would have happened to both of them if Mike hadn't joined her class. The possibilities made her shiver.

Gemma looked up and took a deep breath. Funny how the water should look so mucky and the air could smell so clean. It was a beautiful afternoon. The sky was becoming overcast and grey, the air was humid and uncomfortable, and yet Gemma had never felt so alert, so alive. Today was the first day of the rest of her life. She'd heard that said before but she'd never really understood it until now.

She could see the pathway beside the canal to the right and the mass of briars, weeds and bushes behind the rubbish which fringed the canal on the left. Just beyond all the foliage were buildings. Houses mostly and tall office blocks behind those. Gemma had never seen anything so wonderful. She risked a shy glance at Mike. He was looking around too. For now they stood in silence – apart but together. It was a strange feeling and Gemma knew it couldn't last. But she was going to make the most of it whilst it did.

'We'd better get back to school,' she sighed.

'I suppose.'

They walked back without saying a word. Once they'd entered the school gates, Gemma said, 'Well, I'll be seeing you.'

'Yeah, OK,' Mike said.

And they walked off in opposite directions just as the buzzer sounded for the end of the lunch break.

48
Mike
Stories

'Robyn, can I talk to you?'

The whole class quietened down. It was the first time in a long while that Gemma had spoken to anyone in the class apart from Mr Butterworth. Mike looked around. All eyes were on Gemma. She was swallowing convulsively like there was something stuck in her throat. Mike saw her look around the classroom, a slow burn of red creeping over her cheeks. She looked almost terrified. What was she doing now?

'What about?' Robyn frowned.

'It's about Mike.'

Mike's heart gave a lurch. A whole day had passed since the ... canal business and Mike had begun to think that Gemma meant it when she said she wouldn't say a word. He should've known better.

'He didn't steal the jumper, he was bringing it out of the shop to show me,' Gemma said. 'He wanted to ask me if I thought his nan might like it for her birthday.'

'But it was stuffed under his jacket ...'

'Only because he thought the shop assistant wouldn't let him take it out of the shop. He was going to pay for it.'

'You don't know that,' Robyn dismissed.

'Yes, I do. He told me so. Besides he wouldn't take anything from your mum's shop. One – he's not a thief. And two – he likes you too much.' Gemma smiled.

Robyn turned to look at Mike – as did everyone else. There were a couple of wolf whistles and some giggles. Mike wanted a ravenous hole to appear under his chair and suck him in! Couldn't Gemma come up with anything better than that?

'He didn't have to steal that jumper from your mum's shop, and I can prove it,' said Gemma. 'He left his money with me. See!' Gemma handed Robyn an envelope.

Robyn reached out and took it. She shook the money out on to the table.

'It's all there. You can count it if you like,' Gemma told her.

'I don't understand.' Robyn's frown was carved around the corners of her mouth. 'How come you've got his money?'

'Because Mike is too embarrassed to tell you what really happened. It was all just a misunderstanding. Mike's not a thief. I was there. I know.'

'You're the girl who ran away when Helen asked you if you knew Mike,' Robyn realised.

'Helen?'

'Mum's shop assistant.'

'Oh. I didn't know that was her name. She looked like some kind of harpy. I took one look at her face and scarpered.' Gemma shook her head. 'It was really cowardly. I should've hung around and told her what was really going on. But honestly, Robyn, that woman looked like she was about to chew a chair leg!'

'Yeah, she can be a bit ferocious!' Robyn agreed drily.

'So I'm sorry about all the hassle. I should've stayed and explained to everyone what was happening.'

'But why didn't Mike say something?' Robyn turned to look at Mike again. 'Mike, you should've just told Mum and Helen what you were up to.'

Mike shrugged, looking helplessly at Gemma.

'He wanted to, but when I ran off he didn't think anyone would believe him. That's why he never said anything, even to the police. And he didn't want to get me into trouble, which makes me feel even worse. That's the kind of person he is.'

'Oh, I see,' Robyn said doubtfully.

Mike stared at her. She wasn't going to believe that load of old guff, was she? But from the tentative smile she was giving him, it seemed that she might.

'I'm really sorry about that. I know I caused a lot of trouble by running away. I didn't mean to,' Gemma said. 'And it wasn't fair to Mike either.'

'It's OK.' Robyn smiled. 'I'll tell my mum.'

Gemma picked up the money and stuffed it back into the envelope. She went back to her table and sat down, her hands and the envelope on her lap. Everyone was watching her. Gemma smiled tentatively.

'Oops! Mike, before I forget, I'd better give this back to you before Mr Butterworth arrives.' She leaned across her table and handed over the envelope.

Mike couldn't believe it. She wasn't really going to give him fifty pounds, was she? He opened the envelope. Inside was one crisp, new-looking five pound note. Somehow she'd managed to pocket the rest! Mike turned in his chair to look at Gemma.

'Is it all there?' Gemma asked.

'Everything you owe me – yes,' Mike replied.

'So we're all square now?'

'Not even close,' Mike whispered.

'No, I guess not,' Gemma said seriously.

Ignoring the speculative look Kane was giving him, Mike turned back to face the front of the classroom.

49

Gemma
To Find Mum

'Dad, can I talk to you?'

Gemma's father looked up from the kitchen table where he was reading his newspaper.

'What is it?'

'First of all, here's the money you lent me.'

Dad took the envelope and counted the notes. 'It's five pounds short,' he said, frowning.

'Yeah, I know. Can I owe you?'

'Looks like I don't have much choice in the matter.' Dad raised his eyebrows. 'So are you going to tell me why you needed to borrow fifty pounds for just one day.'

Gemma shook her head.

'Did it get you out of trouble like you said it would?'

'It helped,' Gemma replied.

Dad sighed. 'I wish I knew what you were up to.'

Gemma shrugged. She sat down opposite him.

'I've got something to tell you, Dad.'

'Oh yes?' Dad folded up his paper and put it on the table before him. 'This sounds ominous.'

Gemma took a deep breath. 'I'm going to look for – and find – Mum.'

'Pardon?'

'I don't mean I'm going to go marching up and down the streets looking for her,' Gemma rushed on. 'But I want you to help me put an ad in the local papers around where we used to live. I'll start that way and take it from there.'

'I see.'

'So are you going to help me?'

'You really want to do this?'

'Yes. And I will, with or without you – but I would like your help.'

'I see.' Whilst her father didn't say yes, Gemma noticed that he didn't exactly say no either.

'And I'd like a favour.'

'I'm not giving you any more money.'

'No, it's not that. I want you . . . Could you tell me about my mum, please?'

Gemma watched as her dad slowly put down his newspaper.

'What d'you want to know?'

'Everything.'

'Fancy a pizza whilst we talk?' Dad said carefully.

'I'd like that.' Gemma smiled.

'D'you want to order one in or shall we go out?'

186

Gemma considered. 'Let's go out.'

'Can I come with you?' Tarwin piped up from behind Gemma, making her jump. 'I'd like to hear this too.'

'How long have you been standing there?' asked Dad.

'Long enough!'

'Don't sneak up on people like that,' Gemma said, annoyed.

'What's the matter? Got a guilty conscience?' Tarwin grinned.

Not any more. At least . . . not so much any more, Gemma thought.

'OK then. Get your jackets and we'll set off,' said Dad.

50

Mike
Something To Tell You

Mike sat on the sofa in between Gramps and Nan. Nan was watching the news. Gramps was reading a historical novel. Mike picked up the remote control and switched off the telly.

'Nan, Gramps, I have something to tell you.' Mike rushed out the words before he could change his mind.

'What is it, dear?' Nan asked.

Silence.

'It's the truth about Mum and Dad and me,' Mike said at last. 'It's the truth about what happened that night.'

Gramps and Nan looked at each other.

'We're listening,' said Gramps slowly.

51

Gemma
Out

It was late by the time Gemma, Tarwin and Dad returned home but it didn't matter. Gemma had more energy than she'd had in a long, long time.

Her dad had given her a lot to think about. He had told her everything, some of which didn't paint him in a very sympathetic light at all. But Gemma had never felt closer to him or her brother. They'd even managed to share a few jokes and smiles. Over the last couple of years they had shared a lot of shouting and unhappiness but this was the first time in a long while that they had shared laughter.

Gemma entered her room and immediately saw her scrapbooks, sitting on top of the wardrobe collecting dust. She stood on her bedroom chair and brought them down in the heaviest piles she could manage. First thing tomorrow she was going to put them all in the dustbin. First thing tomorrow.

Well . . . maybe not scrapbook number seven! That

was the one with all the smiling mums and the happy endings. It would go – but not quite yet. The rest were definitely on their way out!

52

Mike
Suspicions

'So now you know the truth,' Mike said, his head bent.

He'd spent the last half-hour telling his grandparents all about living with Mum and Dad since Dad lost his job, right up the moment where he'd killed his own father and let his mum take the blame for it. Now he waited for the axe to fall. All that was left now was for Gramps or Nan to speak and tell him that he could no longer live under their roof. He waited.

'So now we know,' Nan sighed.

'I thought it was something like that,' said Gramps. 'But before all that trial business, every time we asked your mum how things were, she'd smile and shrug and say fine. I wish she'd trusted us. I wish she'd confided in us. Michael, it was an accident. You must never, ever blame yourself – d'you hear me?'

'She probably thought that because we're Richard's parents, we wouldn't believe her,' Nan said sadly. 'But I knew Richard had changed. After he lost his job, every time I talked to him on the phone he was brusque and impatient. And there was that time we arrived just before Christmas and your mum was in tears.'

Gramps nodded. 'I knew then that things weren't right at your house, but none of you would say a word and we didn't want to interfere. I'll regret that until my dying day.'

Mike looked up with a deep frown. What was going on? 'Don't you understand? Dad's dead because of me. I pushed him. If I'd stopped to call an ambulance or told Mum what had happened, Dad might still be alive today.'

'That's not your fault,' Nan said at once. 'It was an accident. In your shoes I would've probably done the same thing.'

Mike had never believed that it was possible to feel like laughing and crying at the same time, but now he did. He hadn't expected Nan and Gramps to be so . . . understanding. He'd thought they'd only known what had been revealed in court, but they obviously knew a lot more than he'd given them credit for. Gramps moved to sit beside him. To Mike's surprise, he took one of Mike's hands in both of his and smiled sadly.

'When I think of your poor mum pleading guilty to the manslaughter charge so she wouldn't be charged with murder.' Gramps sighed. 'There must be something we can do . . .'

'Mum tried to tell the court about Dad's behaviour and sometimes he did hit her, but Mum would never let anyone know, so it ended up working against her because she had no proof.' Mike shook his head as he remembered all the things, the terrible things, the judge had said about his mum – as if Mum would make up a story like that. If the judge only knew how hard it was for his mum to admit in the first place that everything at home wasn't wonderful.

'I don't know how your mum coped for so long, I really don't,' said Nan. 'I would've upped and left long before she did.'

'But Dad was your *son*.'

'Yes, and we loved him very much and we always will. But that doesn't change what he did to you and your mum,' said Gramps. 'And we could never condone that.'

Mike looked from Gramps to Nan and back again. He didn't trust himself to speak. He had a lump the size of a football in his throat and if he attempted one word, one sound, one murmur, he'd burst into tears.

'We did write to your mum, Mikey,' Nan said gently. 'But your mum blames herself for not getting both of you away sooner. All she wants is the best for you and she reckons that seeing her in prison would upset you too much.'

'But I want to see her. I really do,' said Mike.

'I'll tell you what.' Nan smiled. 'Let's all write to her. Maybe between the three of us we can persuade her that we really want to see her.'

'I don't understand.' Mike could feel tears pricking at his eyes. 'You don't *hate* me?'

'Mike, whatever happened in the past or happens in the future, you're our grandson and we love you,' Gramps told him gently. 'Don't you know that by now?'

Tears spilt out on to Mike's cheeks. Horribly embarrassed, he brushed them away but they wouldn't stop coming. Then Gramps put his arm around Mike's shoulder and hugged him – and Mike knew he wouldn't stop crying for a long, long time.

53

Gemma
Going On

Gemma entered the classroom and started walking to her desk. She slowed when she reached the middle of the room.

'Morning, Robyn and Sarah.' Gemma smiled.

The two girls looked up, stunned.

'Morning,' Gemma repeated.

'Hi!' said Robyn.

'Hello.' Sarah frowned.

Gemma's smile brightened. She walked to her table. On the way she saw Mike. He was already sitting down. She stopped and looked at him. He looked at her. Neither of them said a word. Gemma went to her table and sat down.

Mike dug into his bag to get out his pencil case.

'What's got into Gemma this morning?' Kane whispered to him.

'Maybe she got out of bed on the right side for a change.' Mike shrugged. 'Ouch!'

Gemma had poked him in the back with her ruler. 'I

heard that!' she told them. 'And next time, if you've got something to say about me, say it to my face. OK?'

'Don't be so nosy. We were talking about you, not to you,' Kane told her.

'Well, I'm right behind you. And my ears work.' Gemma turned from Kane to Mike. 'So how are you today?'

'I've been better.' Mike shrugged. 'What about you?'

'I've been worse,' Gemma replied.

Gemma and Mike looked at each other. There were no stars, no sparks, no smiles, but they understood each other. Mike was the first to look away. Gemma sighed. She had a long, long way to go, but she'd taken the first steps. Maybe one day she and Mike could be . . . friends. Maybe one day. Gemma looked around. She was getting curious looks from some others in the class. She smiled at them. They turned away. Gemma sighed again. This was going to take time and a lot of hard work. Her hands twisted and turned in her lap. Now that she no longer had newspapers to read and cut up, she didn't know what to do with herself. Still, that itself was progress of a sort.

'Watch out, world! I'm coming!' Gemma said softly.

Mike turned to give her a puzzled look. 'Did you say something?'

'Yeah!' Gemma replied at once. 'I said, "Watch out, world! I'm coming!" '

Kane and a few others turned at that.

'Gemma, I wonder about you sometimes.' Kane shook his head.

'How sweet! But there's no need to, Kane. I'm fine.' Gemma smiled. 'Or at least, I'm heading that way.' And that was the strange, bizarre, wonderful, glorious truth!

Mr Butterworth entered the classroom – and the lesson began.

A Note from the Author

Tell Me No Lies was inspired by two incidents from my childhood, both of which involved bullying. The first one involved a group of ten-year-old girls (including me, I regret to say) in a bullying incident where we said something incredibly mean to another girl about her family and made her cry. The girl was the class bully and had made the lives of all the girls in the class a misery up until that point, so at the time I tried to justify our behaviour by saying the bully was only getting dose of her own medicine. My maths has never been brilliant, but even I know that two wrongs don't make a right. As I watched the girl in question run off in floods of tears, I swore to myself I'd never be involved in bullying anyone ever again.

The second incident involved a girl in my secondary school who put up with being systematically bullied by three other girls in our class for years before she finally broke down and told someone what was going on. I still remember how shocked I was to hear about the abuse my classmate had had to put up with, not just once or twice but regularly, year in, year out.

Bullying is serious. Recently someone said to me that bullying is 'something every child has to go through at some point and it's part of growing up'. Well, it shouldn't be. Bullying ruins lives. It leaves scars that may never heal. Bullying isn't necessarily physical either. I wanted to write a story about bullying from both the victim and the bully's point of view. And I wanted my story to be about emotional rather than physical abuse. So that's how *Tell Me No Lies* came about.

If you're being bullied, don't keep it bottled up inside. Tell someone – a teacher, a parent/guardian or phone someone who can help, like ChildLine on 0800 1111. ChildLine is a completely free and confidential service.

And if you're bullying someone, stop. Just stop.

About the Author

Malorie Blackman (Children's Laureate 2013–2015) is the author of the multi-award-winning Noughts & Crosses series, which deals with issues of race and relationships. She has written more than sixty books for children and teenagers, including *Pig-Heart Boy*, which was shortlisted for the CILIP Carnegie Medal and adapted into a BAFTA-winning television series. Blackman is particularly celebrated for writing about a diverse range of characters, including those who are often marginalized in society, such as teenage fathers in her novel *Boys Don't Cry*. In 2008 she was honoured with an OBE for her services to children's literature.